Handsome Men
Are Slightly
Sunburnt

∫

SCEPTRE

Handsome Men Are Slightly Sunburnt

FRANK RONAN

SCEPTRE

Copyright © by Frank Ronan 1989, 1990, 1992, 1993,
1994, 1995, 1996

First published in 1996 by Hodder and Stoughton
A division of Hodder Headline PLC
A Sceptre Book

The right of Frank Ronan to be identified as the Author of
the Work has been asserted by him in accordance with the
Copyright, Designs and Patents Act 1988.

10 9 8 7 6 5 4 3 2 1

A CIP catalogue record for this title is available from the British
Library.

ISBN 0 340 66074 0

Typeset by Palimpsest Book Production Limited,
Polmont, Stirlingshire
Printed and bound in Great Britain by
Mackays of Chatham PLC, Chatham, Kent

Hodder and Stoughton
A division of Hodder Headline PLC
338 Euston Road
London NW1 3BH

∫

Contents

$\int$

SALTHILL

∫

He felt as though he were becoming a shadow, fading away as the child grew larger within her; as his role in her life became less significant. Before she had become pregnant they had had a sort of loose equality. They had been students in Cork, living on yoghurt and cigarettes in term time and camping in Europe for the summers. If it had not been for the conception they might well have been engaged to be married by now, in spite of Ron's anarchic leanings. But, as it was, the expected arrival of the child seemed to have set a date for their sundering. She had arranged for an adoption, and arranged it so that there would be no room for Ron in her subsequent life. It was her decision, and that of her parents. The chain of events was out of his control and he was only a shadow in the spectacle.

They had never been deep. They had never said the I love you stuff and extracted promises in all the years they had been inseparable. Their conduct had been guided by instinct. In their backgrounds there had been no rules or precedents for their lifestyle. Their parents had been the sort of people who had resorted to the rosary to ward off the temptations of sex during courtship. So Ron and Josy had led a double life, going to Mass when they were at home in the country, and smoking dope and sleeping together when they were in the city. None of this seemed unnatural to them. It was a way of life for our whole generation.

The discovery that Josy was pregnant had coincided with Ron being offered a job working with computers in Galway. He calmed down his punk image and took the job to support them. Her parents, once they had stopped screaming, helped her to think the whole thing out rationally. Of course, abortion was never considered. A shotgun wedding was out of the question because they considered themselves to be the sort of family to whom that kind of thing did not happen. And they had never approved of Ron in the first place. The plan was that Josy was to go away quietly and not come home until she had had the child adopted, and then she could pick up her life again and no more would be said.

Ron and Josy found a flat in Galway, near the centre. It had small rooms and high ceilings and few windows. Josy spent almost her entire time sitting in this flat, waiting it out with a sort of bovine placidity. She smoked a lot to pass the time, in spite of Ron's objection that it would harm the health of the child. She refused to think of the child as a person, and so could not believe that it had health to be damaged. Sometimes he would go home to the country to spend the weekend with his parents, and then she would always make sure that he left some dope with her so that she could deal with her immobility. She would creep out on Saturday morning and spend all the money he had left her on junk food, and then stay in bed eating and smoking until he came back.

While he was away, and had to spend nights without her, he could feel the process of his fading away accelerate, until he could look down sometimes and not be sure if he could see himself. His significance to himself had become so grey that if he passed a mirror he could almost be certain afterwards that he had not seen his own reflection. He had not told his family about Josy's expectancy, and so he could only spend the weekend sitting in whichever room was empty, working out sentences to say to her and resolutions to their sadness. Then he would leave the farm and arrive back in Galway, and there she would be, sitting in bed in squalor, huge and delicate with child, and as pleased to see him as though she might love him. Then he could think of none of the sentences he had imagined. Everything he could say would fall away from him.

Sometimes he could look at her and see last year's nineteen-year-old girlfriend disguised as a pregnant woman. Consumed in pregnancy. Sometimes he would see a woman he had never known, and he couldn't remember if he had ever loved her. Nor could he work out whether the amount of pain she was causing him at that moment was an indication that he loved her still. Often she would smile at him, with real pleasure in his company, and he would respond to those smiles. But he could never make himself unaware of her ultimate determination to be rid of him and the child.

On a Thursday, when she was eight months gone, he came home in the evening, wet with summer rain. As usual there was little food in the flat; no more than a few potatoes. He cooked them for her and they had potatoes and butter and tea. They ate in silence, but sometimes she would laugh at something known to herself alone, and he would smile at her in pathetically attempted empathy. Afterwards he cleared the plates into the sink while she sat and hummed to herself. The sink smelled a little, because they washed dishes as they needed them and not as they used them, and there were dishes at the bottom of the sink which had lain there since the day they moved in.

Later on, Bernard O'Dowd, who shared the flat with them in an unobtrusive way, came home and brought some cider with him. They sat in the other room to drink it. Bernard was morose and silent, as usual, and the television had broken, so they chainsmoked and listened to the pelting rain.

This was their sitting room, but it was also the room

where Bernard slept, and it might have struck you as odd that, even if you looked carefully, there was no evidence of Bernard's inhabitancy to be seen. You could assume that he slept on the sofa, which at this moment was occupied by Ron and Josy, she with her head deep in his lap (while Bernard sat on a cushion by the wall), but there were no bedclothes, no odd socks, nor any shred of territorialism in Bernard's attitude. He looked mostly at his own hands, as if he might be considering their ugliness, and glanced up the odd time at Ron and Josy. But he never let his eye be caught.

Occasionally, Josy would break the silence by saying something to Ron. It was always a question, and she always prefixed it, in her whining voice, with his Christian name (and as she did it he would feel a loathing for his own name).

'Ron,' she would say, 'can we go to Salthill on Saturday?'

Usually he would agree to whatever she asked. Then she would bury her head deeper in his lap and tighten her arms around him. He would try not to stiffen, try to tolerate her embrace, even though he felt it was wrong that, while mentally and emotionally they were drifting further apart, physically their love was more urgent than ever. It made him uncomfortable to have this degree of intimacy with someone who felt like a stranger. He resented his lust for her and he felt diminished by the physical comfort she took in him.

After one of her questions he found himself flushed with an anger. But there was something in him that would not direct the anger at her, and it is difficult to be angry with something that hangs on to you in a way that makes it seem part of you, rather than a parasite. As the anger in him formed itself into a stab, he found that he was directing it across the room, towards Bernard. In another moment the sight of Bernard irritated him, and he could feel a dry, cutting remark at the back of his throat, ready to be launched. 'Well, Bernard, nothing to say for yourself tonight?' But he never said it. Bernard had looked up, off his guard, and their eyes had caught each other out.

It took Ron a few of the minutes that followed to work out the significance of the expression he had caught on Bernard's face, but once he had thought it through and resolved it the logic of it seemed impeccable. For a long time he had assumed that Bernard's silence was a sort of repression. He had wondered once if Bernard wasn't in love with Josy, but a little observation had scotched that idea. Now the truth began to seep through, with the robustness of a newly realised truth.

The notion that Bernard was in love with him flattered him into laughing out loud, shaking with laughter in a mildly hysterical way. Josy, in his lap, said nothing, only kept her place on his quivering thighs. Bernard O'Dowd said nothing either, but he looked out at Ron from time to time, from beneath his eyelids and through the cigarette smoke, and he blushed a bit but, seemingly, more out of pleasure than embarrassment.

When the short burst of laughter had subsided, and a while had passed, and the room was back in stillness as though it had never happened, Josy whimpered a question at him again.

'Ron,' she said, 'will you promise me something?'

She spoke in a rural drawl, dropping the corners of her mouth in an ugly way as if she were about to cry, but it was only the way that all the girls of her parish spoke, whether they were happy or miserable.

He thought about her question for a while, because it puzzled him. It was seldom that she used that figure of speech; that she asked him to promise her something. He decided that she was trying to re-establish her position in the wake of his burst of laughter. He couldn't see that the question was anything but a put-down. He resigned himself to her next question and answered her last one.

'What?' he said.

'Ron,' she said, 'can we get some drugs with the wages tomorrow? Some really good ones before it's all gone?'

She spoke of the drugs with the guilelessness and innocence of a girl from up the country, but to such an extent that it seemed affected. She always did this: treated drugs as if they were Smarties, making as much distinction between dope and acid as you might between a red and a yellow sweetie. He used to find it charming, but since her pregnancy it terrified him. Even so, he could find nothing in himself to fight her with.

'I suppose so,' he said. He could see that her existence in this flat was a long dull sentence; that she might need the odd blast of something to keep her going. He felt he could do with a lift himself.

'Do you promise?' she said. 'Will you buy drugs for me before it's all spent.'

'What about the Tiddler?' he asked her. That was his only weapon. She hated it when he called the child the Tiddler; when he called it into being with a name. He had been unaware, in the beginning, that it was a need to anthropomorphise his own child, and now that he knew how much it irritated her he tried not to do it so often, but the name came out at these moments. Even still, when it came out it was not remonstrant, but only in the low, appeasing voice that he used with her these days. He wondered, as he spoke, if he hadn't always used this voice for her, but he couldn't remember now.

She snapped, as she would, 'Don't call it the Tiddler.'

He said nothing.

She was smoking so much that the child would be lucky to be born alive in any case. He wished that she would take her head out of his lap; plugged into him like a tick or mistletoe; and the Tiddler plugged into her, each of them behaving as though they would never survive without their host. And the plan was that after another month of this none of them would ever need to see the others again.

He had forgotten about Bernard, but now Bernard sneezed and was blowing his nose with his huge hands around a handkerchief. Ron began to smile again, because the idea that Bernard was in love with him was such light relief; such a dazzling red herring. Bernard wanted him, and he wanted the Tiddler and Josy, and the Tiddler wanted Josy, and no one could have anybody. And Josy wanted nobody at all, but to begin her life again as though this one had never happened, and to do this she was prepared to use whoever was available. Bernard sat across the room in silence, pretending to be wrapped in his own thoughts, but watching them carefully. Ron almost began to laugh again. This time his laugh would have had a note of desperation in it, but Josy prevented that by speaking again. Her voice had returned to its wheedling mode and sulky country accent.

'Ron,' she said, 'will you? Will you promise? Go on, say you will.'

He acquiesced. He couldn't begin an argument that would focus on the child, not while she denied its humanity. She was determined that, although she was temporarily incarcerated by this pregnancy, she would treat it as an illness, to be cured by adoption. There were times when she behaved as though the child had injured her, and she should have no conscience about injuring it in return.

Having got the assurance she wanted from him she began to whimper that she was tired and that it was time for bed. At that moment, going to bed with her was the last thing he could imagine. The thought of all that damp warmth and breathing made him shudder with revulsion. He needed to extricate himself from her. He found himself issuing a command to Bernard.

'We'll go out,' he heard himself say.

They left her to her bed and went out on Bernard's small

motorbike. Ron sat side-saddle on the back because his trousers were too tight to put his leg across. They were stopped in Ayre Square by a Garda who said that it was illegal to ride that way. After that, Ron had to sit further back, with his knees together like a jockey. It was late and the pubs were shut, so Ron told Bernard to go to the beach, and Bernard obeyed.

While they rode, to amuse himself and to take his mind off Josy and the Tiddler and his irritation with the Garda, Ron held an imaginary conversation with Bernard, in which he tried to be honest and compassionate. It was something that he often did, pretending to himself that he was as good and wise as God's first cousin. He could do it most easily in the dark, and he found it impossible to do if he had just caught sight of his face in the mirror. The evidence of inadequacy and deception on his own features was too much for him.

In this unspoken conversation he reminded Bernard that he had known him for four years, and watched him stumble in and out of girls' lives with his huge ungainly frame, but it wasn't until that night that he had realised the truth. He admitted that he was more flattered than anything to have someone in love with him; that it was a relief to think it was possible to be loved by someone. He explained that he had laughed, not because he found Bernard's love ridiculous, but at the pleasure of being loved at all. He said that he wished he had Bernard's courage; the courage to fall in love with someone himself.

As the motorbike struggled along, he crouched in the lee of Bernard's back, knowing that they must look outrageous: an anally retentive giant and a small punk on the same minuscule bike. He realised that, even if he were to become good and wise, he could never have that honest conversation with Bernard in real life. It would break the man in two. It was possible that, even though he was in love, Bernard was unaware of it himself. You cannot underestimate the simplicity of another man's mind or self-deceptions.

And what if Bernard were not in love at all? Would it be worth losing a good friend for the sake of a stab at honesty?

They arrived at the beach, and for two hours or so they wandered among the rocks and stones. There was no rain now, but stars here and there, and an orange glow out from Galway. It was turning out to be a cold night for the time of year, but it seemed a blessing not to be rained on.

They talked about music, which seemed to be the only subject they ever talked about. But this time there was some animation in the way that Bernard spoke. His sentences seemed longer and his opinions more definite. Ron wondered if this was something that proved his new theory, or whether it was something which he imagined in the light of his new theory. There was a moment when Bernard sat heavily on a large, damp boulder and Ron stood in front of him and, for a long time, they just looked at each other. That had never happened before. When they broke off the look Ron knew, by the way that Bernard was at once flattered and embarrassed, that he had been right about the love, and right also not to mention it.

Once he was certain about Bernard it stopped being an amusement to him and began to be a burden. What was he to do about it? There would be guilt for Bernard's suffering, and guilt for not being able to reciprocate. His mood changed to leaden despair, and he told Bernard to ride home without him. He would walk. Bernard obeyed.

Walking back to the flat took a long time, and it began to rain again when he was about halfway there. Even in the orange and pink street lighting and the filthy downfall of rain, Galway still looked the same sterile grey colour that it always had; still exuded the same impersonal, clean charm. But walking by himself worked; had the effect he had been after. By the time he was back at the flat he felt that he had faded away almost completely, and that there was nothing left of him but the ache in his knees from walking and the stream of cold rain down his spine.

Josy was awake for him. Bernard had vanished into the sitting room and there would be no evidence of him until morning. He was never heard to snore or toss or fart, although the partition wall between their room and his was paper-thin. In the morning there would be no sign that he had stayed in the flat at all.

Perhaps that was why Josy felt no embarrassment for the noise she always made in their lovemaking. Perhaps she failed to recognise the existence of Bernard at night. These nights she made love to Ron for hours on end, regardless of the child she was carrying. He was surprised by his own stamina, but there was something about her wildness and urgency that kept him excited, no matter how much his cold mind thought that it was laughable. If he felt disgust, from time to time, he found that he could detach himself from his physical thrashings and the greed with which she was consuming him. And it might have been that the idea that she was destroying him acted as a catalyst to his libido. He kept thinking that she was trying to wring every last drop from him and leave him dead and dry. He watched himself gallop towards his own dehydration.

That night, while they fucked, he thought of Bernard in the next room, surely awake in all the noise, and listening; possibly taking his own pleasure from it, even if it might be torture to him. Sometimes he thought of stopping, for Bernard's sake, but he was always caught up in Josy's compulsion.

Once, he had the dangerous notion that he was not making love to Josy so much as to the Tiddler.

The next day, Friday, after he had stopped work and put his computer terminal to bed, he collected his wages. He and Bernard met, on the way home, as they often did, and came in together. There was a ritual which they performed every Friday, which transformed Ron from the respectable person he had to present at work into the true, anarchic self which he had to reserve for moments of freedom. Bernard maintained the same appearance, weekday or weekend. It would seem that he would have you think he was a trainee accountant both outside and within.

Bernard would wash Ron's hair for him. Ron had never thought about it before, but now, as he leaned over the basin, he became aware of the tenderness with which the big man was pulsing his fingers in his scalp, and he became aware that this was the closest Bernard got, or was likely to get, to a consummation of his love.

Looking sideways through the falling suds and the open bathroom door, he could see Josy basking on the sofa; watching them and smiling at them, as though they were performing for her. He found that he could remember what it was like to be in love with her. He remembered now that she had loved him once, and that had something to do with the way that Bernard was massaging his hair. He could remember her being tender, and her waiting to hear a good word from him, and her smiling after their eyes would meet. Once he could remember all that, he knew that it was dead, and that the baby had destroyed it. Rather than hate the baby for it, he still wanted to keep the baby, as the one thing that might be salvaged from it all.

On the other hand, he could see her point of view. She had to get rid of them all and stand on her own two feet. How would she know what a moral suicide was? What evidence had she that she was killing the good within her?

Now, she stayed on the sofa, entertained by them after a day of staring at the walls; happy at the prospect of a weekend with a bit of company, and maybe a snort of something nice to get her out of herself.

Ron dried his hair, and Bernard helped him to put it up in spikes with glue and hairspray. It hurt Bernard to do this because he had washed the hair with such love and Bernard, having the soul of a conservative, liked things to be clean and normal. But Bernard was loyal too and, despite the pain it caused him, he worked the comb and glue until Ron was satisfied, and said nothing.

Ron said that they would go to Salthill that evening, and Josy whined because she had wanted to go to Salthill the next day and spend that evening smoking drugs, but Ron persuaded her by saying that Salthill was where he needed to go to buy the drugs. And then she sulked a little and they had to charm her and tease her as you would with a child, and at one moment Ron even went to the trouble of sitting on Bernard's shoulders while they sang 'Slaney Valley' to her, and then she clapped her hands in a childish way and demanded that they do it again.

In Salthill it was another long rainy summer evening and they wandered from one amusement arcade to another, where Ron pumped money into the one-armed bandits, sometimes working two or three at a time, while Bernard stood beside him, watching the fruit symbols revolve as though his life depended on it. Josy spent her time at the penny grab, trying to win a Toblerone.

Ron had some spectacular wins, but all the money would get swallowed again, and after a time there was no money left at all. When it was gone, he and Bernard went out and sat on bollards on the other side of the road, by the sea, leaving Josy to play with the penny grab.

They sat with their backs to the bay, watching the arcades and the people in them. Ron's hair subsided slowly in the drizzle. He became aware of Bernard's voice talking beside him, and he was so astonished to hear sentence after sentence of it that he forgot to take in what was being said. It was something about a children's book that Bernard had thought of writing, about a man who tried to own the sea and was drowned.

'But not this sea,' Bernard said, glancing back at the grey water behind him. 'My own sea, at home.'

That Bernard should have such a soul was disturbing to Ron, even though he knew he should be glad of it. It made him feel inadequate, and guilty for not having a soul himself. So it was a relief to see Josy walking across the road towards them, and to hear Bernard's voice dwindle as she came nearer.

As she walked, he could see nothing of her, only the lump attached to the front of her, and the horror of all their futures became clear to him. He could see the resentments and the breakdowns, and he had a premonition of that moment, five years later, when he went completely mad and tore his eyebrows out. He could see Josie as a junkie and the Tiddler growing up snug and unhappy among people who had been too neurotic to live without children. Given all the destruction that was to occur in the wake of this baby, he knew that it would be sensible to hate it. If he could, somehow, cauterise the way in which he loved this creature there might be a chance of saving his sanity. But his love for the child was something that was beyond him and his control, and he had faded to a thing that was only a shadow.

Josy said, 'I need more money for the grab. I nearly have the Toblerone.'

He said, 'The money's gone.'

'Never mind,' she said. 'We'll get the drugs now.'

He said, 'The money's gone.'

She only looked at him. She said nothing about promises. If she was swamped in disappointment she hid it well. Perhaps, in these moments, when it might seem that he had won a tiny battle, she only had to think a month ahead; to think of signing those papers and her freedom, to preserve her equanimity.

They began to walk back towards Galway in the evening drizzle. Bernard was as silent as if he had never spoken.

Josy's burden made her walk with a slow grace. Ron
was thinking that he wasn't shadow enough; that he
was surrounded and crowded out by this friend and this
girlfriend and this child. He had no idea how to overcome
them and become a real person. The only solution he could
see was to fade away and have no significance at all.

∫

HOOK HEAD

5

I never laughed like that until after the wedding. I never broke out, in the middle of nothing, with the free, broad laugh of a madman before our union was a fact of law. There is nothing I can do about it now. I find myself deliriously and unnaturally happy. I catch my eye in mirrors and giggle without dignity.

I suppose I was happy enough before Julia married me, in the two years that we lived together by the sea. She had three children from previous entanglements; from other men who had burnt out in her sphere of influence. I enjoyed the company of the children, though I had never hankered for children of my own. The horrors of the pink wrinkled stage were too much to contemplate. In the case of the three boys I came into them just as they were reaching the intelligent, chatty stage, which is more rewarding. Most of the time they could treat me as an overgrown older brother. I left the authority stuff to her.

God knows how the wedding came about. There was no pressure on us to be married. The idea evolved, and it would have seemed churlish to deny everyone a party, so I evolved along with it.

Once it happened, it was an idyllic wedding. Julia has a good eye. The boys were pages and she herself wore a dress the colour of faded hortensias. I wore my grandfather's morning coat, which was a little mothy and small, but Julia gave me an embroidered silk waistcoat and told me I looked like a peacock. I went to the glass to see and, indeed, the man who looked back was as handsome as ever.

The church was in County Waterford, but we had the breakfast in a Martello tower out by Hook Head, and so there was a long drive from one to the other, by glimpses of the sea, in winter sunshine. We ate, looking out over the water, a long table of gorgeous people, toasting ourselves. There was something medieval in it. And the sea was an extraordinary colour, which I have never seen since. It is not a colour I could easily describe to you.

It was my mother who had driven me to church that morning. She had insisted on it, elbowing the best man out of the way. Near the end of the journey she drew the car up on a back road and turned to me. Her head was still, and her hands were shaking, with determination.

'Now, Michael,' she said.

My mother is an awkward woman at the best of times, and she expresses herself awkwardly. This morning she was almost twisted with awkwardness.

To be honest, I am not sure that the influence of my mother on my life has been wholly benign. I bleed for my poor father, God rest him, but then he was a dreadful man whom you wouldn't wish on any woman.

There is no distance in this world like the gap across a handbrake. From the other side of it I could see that my mother had the look of a mad chicken about her: a sign that she was being serious. I gazed back into her face without catching her eye, a trick I had learned in infancy.

'Now, Michael. I have the whole thing organised. Aiden Connors is waiting for you at Waterford Airport with his little plane. You could be sunning yourself in Andalusia this afternoon and no one will know where you are. I can deal with things here and let you know when things have died down and it's safe for you to come back.'

Perhaps, if she had said it in another way, she might have

convinced me. No, but maybe if it had been someone other than her making the proposition, I might have accepted. I was shaking with apprehension that morning, and longing to be rescued. Anyone could have yanked me out of there and off to Andalusia, except the woman who had orchestrated all the greatest disasters of my youth. I wasn't going to let my mother rescue me when one of my reasons for getting married was to rescue myself from her.

Without hesitating, I said, 'Mother, drive on.'

'Do you realise what you are doing?'

'Do you want me to drive?' I asked.

Aiden Connors turned up at the breakfast and sat at the end of the table looking sheepish. My mother ignored him. I winked at him.

Julia bent towards me and whispered, 'I don't like that man.'

'There's no harm in him,' I said.

The first night of the honeymoon was to be spent in London, between flights. To make the best of it somebody had lent us a barge on Regent's Canal. There had been debate about taking the boys with us but, in the end, we decided to make it as much like a conventional honeymoon as possible. Champagne and embarrassment and, eventually, tropical palms. But the night on Regent's Canal was the worst night of my life.

In spite of I don't know how many hundreds of times of making love in two years of living together, I can honestly say that we seemed to be doing something for the first time that night. We were plunged in emotion. She wept and I wept and the earth might have moved if we weren't on a boat. It was the only time I can think of when that act was so overwhelming that it made sense to me.

I thought it was stunning that marriage, which I had dismissed until then as a formality, should make such a difference to things. It could have been this observation which was partly to blame for what happened later.

It was after we had drawn apart. I reached towards her face with my hand. I was bursting with that self-indulgent emotion which has often been mistaken for love. And there was an aesthetic element too: I thought that she looked extraordinary.

'Don't,' she snapped. 'I have cystitis.'

Then she began to weep in torrents. I should have been able to predict it, of course. She always gets cystitissy and emotional when she drinks too much champagne. It is an allergy, I think. Normally I can be philosophic and supportive about it, but on that night I was thrown into a black misery. I thought that something had been stolen from me.

It is, I believe, quite a normal reaction to a marriage, for a man: to feel that you have been duped. In your imagination the soft consent on the altar conceals a shriek of triumph. Now that she had me in her grasp everything had changed and she no longer gave a toss for me. I felt that I couldn't stay on that boat with her another moment.

I spent most of that night walking the streets. An instinct drew me towards the river. I climbed Ladbroke Grove with the insomniac dog walkers and crossed Earl's Court as the rent boys were shutting up shop for the night. As I walked, an inescapable blackness drew in on me. I thought my end had come. When I got to the river I was terrified to go to the bank and look down into it. I knew that once I saw the water I would drown myself. I stayed north of the embankment, but followed the river from Chelsea to Tower Bridge without glimpsing it or killing myself, and so made the second big mistake of the day.

When I got back to Julia, the morning after that living nightmare, she behaved as though nothing had happened. She carried on as if we had spent the night curled in one another's arms. Once, a long time afterwards, I tried to bring the subject up, but she silenced me by implying that I must have been up to no good on my ramble; that she was, selflessly, prepared to overlook whatever debauchery had defiled the first night of our marriage. What can I say now? If she is going to think that I was being buggered on our wedding night, then the whole episode is best forgotten. I know when not to dig myself in deeper.

To be honest, once the tropical palm part of the honeymoon was over, the marriage was not a success. I felt trapped, and thought about nothing but escape. I probably knew that escape was impossible, but there was something in me that enjoyed planning it anyway.

Julia treated me as she treated all things which came into her possession. She is loyal to her possessions. Once she has seen a thing handsome enough to covet she doesn't rest until she owns it. And then it is left to gather dust with everything else in her collection. If there is a threat from the outside she becomes a monstrous defender, but anything safely in her domain is left to wither. Indeed, since a thing is less likely to be stolen if it doesn't look as handsome as it might, it may be that she encourages a coating of dust and a few wrinkles as an anti-burglar device.

So, I came to feel as though I was a good-looking piece of furniture, sagging in her bedroom. But keeping a husband is more complicated than keeping a chest of drawers, and she had her work cut out, screaming at me for every minor transgression I was accused of making. I drank before I met her, I'll admit – but living with her didn't make me feel like giving it up.

But then, none of that is the whole truth either, or even a substantial part of it. There were other factors. I began to make a lot of money soon after we were married. That knocked her off her perch a bit. Until then she had always been made to feel secure by having more money than me. She liked to feel that she was in control, I think, even when she wasn't. I don't know if that was the truth of it either.

Mostly, it was the boys who prevented me from running away. I am a better parent to them than she ever was.

They never heard a bedtime story before my coming; they never knew that adults were capable of playing games with them. Julia has an old hippy idea that children can rear themselves. You might think that, when they come in from school, she would be happy to see them, or ask what they had been doing for the day. But all they ever get is that pre-menstrual scowl and the ante-pyrotechnic silence. They come slinking on to me for a bit of humanity.

And Mother: my mother and Julia were never great friends. Julia had bellowed and raged when she found out about the escape plan my mother had proposed on the way to the church. I suppose it wasn't tactful to tell her about it on the wedding night, but still. Aiden Connors has been banned from our house since.

It was hell whenever my mother came to stay; she and Julia both straining themselves in polite silence; Julia hissing and my mother looking wounded. After my mother's departure the days of repression would result in a huge torrent of screaming, all at once. I would try to creep away and find someone sane to have a drink with: Aiden Connors, for instance. When I got home from an outing she would be waiting with more abuse, but I always came home.

There came a time when I went off drinking with Aiden while my mother was still in the house. I had to phone home at three in the morning to be collected. My car was upside down in a ditch. Aiden and I had been sitting on the chassis, laughing our heads off, to begin with. Then we had to walk two miles to a telephone box. It was my mother who answered the phone – like the old days again.

I have to admit to feeling a touch of nostalgia as she bellowed down the phone at me. That had been the normal routine between us, before Julia. My mother loved to be picking up the pieces of a disaster. Perhaps that is why she caused so many.

She boxed my ears after we had dropped Aiden off. Me,

a man of thirty-five. And I still had Julia's thumping to look
forward to.

Julia was a far more subtle beater of men than my
mother. When I crawled upstairs, after my mother's shrieking lecture, Julia was sitting up in bed with a studied tear or
two dripping down her cheekbones. I remember thinking
that she looked rather glamorous. I undressed, and sat in
bed beside her. Then she unleashed herself, lashing and
clawing at me. I grabbed her wrists and tried to hold her
at arm's length. She began to hiss.

'You're hurting me. You are hurting my wrists. Let me
go or I'll scream.'

'Business as usual,' I said, not letting go.

With a bellow she lunged her head at me and caught
me a glancing blow on the jaw, and then she collapsed,
whimpering as if I had beaten her.

I must have fallen asleep, because the next thing I
remember is seeing Julia sitting in the morning light,
before the glass, examining her face for bruising. She had
an air of disappointment about her. I kept up a pretence
of sleep.

She rose and went into the next bedroom and sat on my
mother's bed for an hour, while they discussed me. The
experience they had shared led to the discovery that they
had plenty in common: in their feelings for me. I could hear
most of their talk through the chimney breast, and I lay in
bed for the duration and heard myself patronised. For some
reason I began to giggle.

The first time that she noticed me laughing at nothing
was some while later. It was in the middle of the night
and it would have appeared that I was asleep. I had been
asleep, but I had woken myself by laughing. Because I had
no way of explaining myself, I pretended to be unconscious.
The noise had woken her. She had been sleeping badly and
fitfully the past while and, if anything, I should think she
was grateful to be woken from her dreams of abstract

displacement. I could sense her turning her pillow over so that the cold side was next to her face. She lay in the moonlight, watching me laugh. I knew what expression was on her face.

She might have forgotten the incident or, to be more accurate, she might have ignored it, if she had not heard the same roar of laughter coming from my office the following afternoon. She came rushing through the house as if I had given a scream for help, and she stood in the doorway, out of breath and looking rather foolish, for once in her life. I was sitting in an eruption of papers and books and pencils. I began to dial a telephone number, ignoring her entrance.

She hated that most; she hated anything that excluded her. Sometimes, if I was talking on the telephone, she would yank the plug out of the wall to draw attention to herself. But now she needed five minutes to catch her breath, and study me calmly, and think of rational explanations.

For the first time since I had known her I felt in possession of myself. It would have been hard for me not to look smug, so I didn't bother trying. She slipped into the chair across the desk from me, like a schoolgirl, in the headmistress's office.

I put the phone down, and caught a glimpse of myself reflected in her eye, and it seemed to me that I had grown more handsome lately. She looked at me closely, sensing that, although I was looking in her direction, I was seeing something else.

'I look like a turnip today,' she said, in a miserable way.

That was a clever move, but I wasn't falling for it. Julia couldn't look like a turnip if she wore mud. I kept my eyes focused on the reflection of myself; me pulsating with health and fitness and function. She changed tactics and asked me what I had been dreaming about the night before.

'Nothing,' I said. 'Why?'

'You laughed out loud.' She was unable to prevent herself

from smiling at the memory of it. That was easy for me to ignore; I never thought she looked her best when smiling.

'I never remember my dreams,' I said.

As I said it a huge smile spread across my face, cancelling out that smile of hers. We both knew that I was famous for remembering the details of my dreams. She tried to smile again, but my happiness and the small lie were excluding her. I had won a battle for the first time in our marriage.

More and more, I began to laugh for no reason. Not only in my sleep, but at any time of the day. I could laugh hugely in the middle of a banal conversation, leaving her floundering and feeling humourless. I would even laugh during sex: sometimes in mid-act; more often just afterwards. In between the loud laughs there were these smiles, suggesting that I knew something she didn't.

It may seem trivial, but I feel that I am winning. I am beating her by exclusion. I laugh because she doesn't know why I laugh. And the boys are catching on. It used to be that all four of us would shrivel as she screamed at us. The other day we all began to laugh, and it was she who shrivelled, like a celluloid witch melting into a grease spot on the floor. I can feel sorry for her now, because one can be magnanimous in victory. She thinks there must be madness somewhere in this house, but she can't be sure whether it is in her or in me.

∫

KILBRIDE

While Michelle Kelly chopped vegetables in the kitchen, and Michelle Kelly's mother chainsmoked before the noon soap opera at the end of the kitchen table, Helen Flood stood outside, at the foot of the ladder which supported Michael Hanlon in espradrilles and loose shorts.

He said, 'It's bloody amazing. I never believed it. I've been in love before, but I thought that love like this only existed in books: when you wake up in the night and spend four hours just watching someone's face. I didn't think it could happen to me. Did you know that this could happen?'

Helen Flood said, 'I suppose I did. I suppose I believed in overwhelming love. But I've never believed that it could last. In the same way that you can believe in God, without necessarily thinking he's that intelligent.'

By looking up, as she spoke, among the shadows up the leg of his shorts, she could distinguish his balls knocking against his thigh when he moved.

'I can see your balls from here,' she said.

'Oh shut up,' he said. But she could see that he had been amused by her observation. She didn't know how to interpret that. She would have liked to think that it meant his new love was not so overwhelmingly pure that it excluded his old enjoyment of ribaldry. Yet she feared, and it was more likely to be the truth, that he now regarded her more as an old friend than as an ex-lover, and saw no danger in foul talk between them.

She had driven here in anger and loneliness, with a confrontation in mind. She had arrived at this house in Kilbride determined to know if she was still loved, in any way, by Michael Hanlon, or whether she had ever been loved by him at all. When her car drew up she looked at the small, slovenly house and the haggard scratched by chickens of poverty and the row of blown modern roses, planted with no attempt to mitigate their vulgarity; when she saw all this she heard her grandmother's voice asking what else you could expect of a girl of that class, a girl out of a cottage by the side of the road?

Her grandmother had never approved of Michael Hanlon. 'None of his family were any good, and there's no reason why he should be.' If Granny had a reason for disliking him it may have been because she seemed to know everyone's secrets, by instinct; by the tone of people's voices. She had always suspected that there was something going on between Helen and Michael. She had greeted every scrap of gossip about him, including the latest story that he had run away with Michelle Kelly, by saying with a triumphal snort, 'It wasn't off the grass he licked it.'

Helen got out of the car, leaving thoughts of her grandmother behind her and, looking at the house again, wondered with intentional unkindness whether the place had a bathroom in it.

She slammed the car door, unnecessarily, and Michael's voice called to her from the other side of the haggard, 'Helen! I'm over here.'

She walked towards the voice, away from the house, relieved that she wouldn't have to knock at the door and explain herself to whatever might answer it.

'Where?' she said, as she pushed her way through the ash plants and the ragwort. 'I can't see you.'

He was up to his thighs in a stream, wearing only shorts,

shaded from the August sun by the leaves of the ash trees which, in that light, were reflecting the undulations of the water like the roof of a cave. He looked thinner and fitter than she had ever seen him and, she thought, handsome. In all the years they had been lovers she had never considered him worth looking at. He had had other qualities. The irony of him seeming handsome to her now was more than she could bear to think about.

He had been lifting rocks to dam the river where it narrowed, and now he was scooping mud from the bottom with a bucket and dumping it beyond the dam.

'What do you think of the new swimming pool?' he asked.

She didn't say anything, because the anger she had come with had gone away and she was in a state of deflation. But she was aware that she was smiling at him and pleased to see him.

'Roll your skirt up,' he said, 'and give us a hand.'

She declined. She hadn't come prepared for such innocent friendliness. She sat on the bank and talked to him.

By the time Michelle Kelly came along they were both laughing hard. He was recounting some new scandal from the town and Michelle Kelly, who had already heard the story, began to laugh with them as soon as she was within earshot. She did not laugh as they did; it was as though she was laughing at their amusement rather than the story itself.

Helen got to her feet and kissed the other woman on the cheek. If there was awkwardness in it, it probably had to do with the fact that Michelle Kelly came from a background where women did not normally kiss each other in greeting.

It was hard to know whether to call her Michelle, or Kelly. When she had first launched herself on a career as a Country & Western singer she had called herself Michelle, but after six months of failure someone had suggested that she use her surname and call herself Kelly. The name-change had been followed by moderate success and, although no one of Helen's acquaintance had ever heard of her before the liaison with Michael, it was said that you could find her records in one or two shops in Waterford. On the covers of these she looked rather more like herself than she managed in real life: a sort of culchie sex kitten, as Helen would have put it. Her band was known as 'Kelly and the Ploughboys'.

Helen decided in favour of calling her Michelle. She knew that she would have to meet the mother. She thought she might laugh out loud if she was in the same room with both of them and had to call one Kelly and the other Mrs Kelly.

Helen wondered if Michael had told Michelle about her: about her years of adulterous lovemaking with him and whether this overwhelming love of his had brought an overwhelming honesty with it. Watching Michelle, she could see no sign of suspicion or jealousy. And, knowing Michael, his idea of honourable behaviour was to say that which caused least trouble and embarrassment to himself. The closest he ever got to truth was silence.

He climbed out of the river and put his wet feet in the espradrilles on the bank.

'Why has your nipple turned grey?' she asked.

He looked at her and down at his nipple with something like alarm. She knew that she shouldn't be watching his body so closely. It was like visiting a house you had once lived in, and looking for changes and faults; looking for reasons to hate the new owner. She wished he had more clothes on; that his body could be hidden from her memories of it.

'It's mud,' he said, wiping it away with the ball of his thumb. And it was only dried mud: the blemish fell as dust, leaving his left nipple identical to his right.

In the house there were photographs of family weddings;

of young men looking uncomfortable and pleased with themselves in hired bow ties; of girls in peach sateen and of Michelle standing among them in scarlet, with the slightly superior air of a Country & Western star consorting with her origins. Helen asked for the bathroom, mostly to vex them because she was convinced that there wouldn't be one, and was shown to a room that was covered in mauve tiles, where the mauve handbasin was shaped like a scallop shell. She collapsed on the lavatory seat and her shoulders shook with silent laughter as she imagined Michael sitting in the mauve and gold bath every morning.

When she emerged Michael was no longer to be seen. She found herself trying to make conversation with Mrs Kelly, who had nicotine-stained hair and wore a tight denim skirt.

'It must be nice and quiet for you out here,' she said, and just at that moment an articulated lorry went past ten yards away on the road and the house shook.

Mrs Kelly seemed not to have noticed. 'I'd rather be in the town,' she said. 'But the Council won't give me a house.'

She dealt Helen an importunate glare as she spoke, knowing that Helen had a brother-in-law who was on the Urban District Council. Helen, not realising this, took the glare as natural animosity and asked where Michael had gone. Michelle said that he was fixing the window at the gable end, and Helen edged in the direction of the door, trying to look as though she was wandering across the room with no purpose. Not that anyone was taking any notice of her. Mrs Kelly had switched on the television at the end of the table, and Michelle was peeling carrots with unwarranted concentration, taking half the flesh away with the skin. Watching Michelle handle and disfigure such phallic objects was more than Helen could bear and she left the house without excusing herself.

She thought she was going mad, and when she got to the foot of Michael's ladder and looked up and saw his pink bollocks swinging in his shorts, she had to think of something banal to say to contain herself.

She wanted to say that this was all very well, this simple idyll, and that he was looking very well on it too, but where did it leave her? She wanted to ask him whether they were still to consider themselves lovers or not.

But she knew the answer already, and she knew that to ask the question would make things awkward between them, so, instead, she said, 'What's wrong with the window?'

He was smearing putty into the cracks in the wood.

'Home improvements,' he said. 'I'm doing the place up for them. The mother-in-law thinks I'm the bees' knees.'

'Mother-in-law?' Helen said it in genuine puzzlement, then realised it was Mrs Kelly he meant, and laughed, derisively.

She noticed that he was not laughing with her. He was concentrating on the putty. She knew him well enough to be alarmed.

She said, 'You aren't serious?'

'About what?'

'You want to marry Michelle?'

He looked at her as though she had asked something preposterous: not as though the question was preposterous in itself, but as though it was something she need not have asked.

'Don't you know?' he said. 'Can't you see it?'

'Marriage?' she said. 'You?'

'I suppose,' he said, with an understanding tone; with a hint of condescension. 'I suppose a lot has happened since I saw you last. A lot has changed. We want to get married: children, the lot. It's like a whole new life since I left Loretta. When I first told Michelle that I loved her and that I was going to leave Loretta for her she just looked at me with tears streaming down her face. Not crying. You can't imagine the intensity of it.'

'Good God,' Helen said.

'I know,' he said, interpreting her horror as amazement. 'It's wonderful. And we have you to thank for it. If it wasn't for you we might never have met.'

Helen could say nothing to this. She winced at his pluralisation of the personal pronoun, a thing he had never done while he lived with Loretta. But she had no need to say anything. He was away on a monologue: a banal, feverous eulogy of his and Michelle's love for each other, while she held the ladder and gazed at his testicles.

Helen declined the offer to stay and have some of the stew for which the carrots had been destined. She drove away feeling impotent, and alarmed to be feeling that way, since a sensation of that kind was not one that she was accustomed to. What impinged on her most was his gratitude to her for putting him in the way of meeting Michelle Kelly. This situation had not been her intention, and she resented being held responsible for an accident, even if the victims were grateful to her.

When, as he saw her to the car, he had thanked her for coming out to visit, he had said to her, 'Thank God you're not a snob. I've a feeling I might be losing a few friends over this one.'

She had smiled complaisantly, but now, alone in the car, at the beginning of a torrent of *esprit de l'escalier*, she said, 'I wasn't, until I met that slut of yours, but I am now.'

A gap-toothed child, standing by the side of the road, saw her talking to herself in the car, and laughed at her, but she didn't see him.

'You bastard,' she said. 'You weak-minded little shit.'

She knew, all the same, that it had been clever of him to make her culpable for his happiness: that it avoided scenes; it allowed him to continue a cosy friendship with her; it prevented her from marring his bliss.

'You're the only person I know,' she said, 'who believes his own lies.'

She counted how many days it had been since he had first clapped his gobshit eyes on Michelle Kelly. Fifteen days. Saturday night to Sunday week.

'Marriage!' she said. 'Marriage?'

It was true that it had been her idea to go to the Starlite Lounge. She didn't know what had possessed her. That Saturday afternoon Fergal, her husband, was watching a soccer match on the television. He was hunched over, fixed on the set, clenching his fists and making little jerks at moments of excitement, muttering encouragement at the players. If she'd had a brick she would have hurled it through the screen.

When Michael phoned he sounded so distraught. He didn't say anything much, but she could hear the desperation in his voice. Loretta had gone to Dublin for the weekend and, although normally he would have been happy to be rid of her for a couple of days, things had been so bad between them lately that he couldn't escape her even when she was a hundred miles away, complaining about him to her friends in Blackrock.

Helen had often told him, with perfect disinterest, that she couldn't understand why he stayed with Loretta. A hen-pecked husband was understandable, in a way, but a hen-pecked boyfriend was a mystery. She often thought that he might have a masochistic streak in him. She had realised, too, that her best interest was served by him staying with Loretta. It was the misery of that relationship which had caused him to need Helen as a lover.

The hunted tone in his voice on the telephone bent her with pity.

'Why don't you come over,' she said, 'and have a bit of supper? No. I have a better idea. We should all go out. The house is driving me mad and we haven't been on the tear for a long while. The paper's here. There must be something on.'

She reached for the local paper and rustled through it

until she came to the entertainments page, and found the advertisement which said that 'Kelly and the Ploughboys' would be appearing at the Starlite Lounge. She read it out loud to him as a joke, and it made him laugh, and then they discussed the other places, but those were all so dreary that they kept coming back to the Starlite Lounge, until it had made the subtle transition from running gag to possibility.

'I've never been there,' she said. 'We could go there for a drink and see what it's like. It might be a laugh. If it's awful we can crawl on somewhere else.'

By the time they had finished talking he was sounding more cheerful. Then she had work to do: persuading Fergal that he wanted to go out, and finding a babysitter.

The Starlite Lounge was a vast, flat-roofed, concrete building. Inside there were acres of mock-Victorian furnishings and etched glass. In the summer night and the throng of young farmers the atmosphere was palpable. Helen, Fergal and Michael stood inside the door and made faces at each other, and would have left straight away, but Helen said that she wanted to go to the Ladies', and disappeared in the direction suggested by the signage. When she returned she said that she had found the original pub that the Starlite had been built onto, hidden at the back of the building, and that they could go and have a drink there.

They had been in the pub for less than half an hour when the band began to play next door, and Michael said he wanted to take a look at it. He hadn't been gone more than three or four minutes when he came back looking flushed and startled.

'I've just seen the girl I'm going to marry,' he said.

Of course, they thought it was a joke. They went to the door to catch a glimpse of Kelly on the bandstand. It was true that she was rather extraordinary looking, but she had a fixed smile, and an odd way of flicking her head to every third bar of the music.

Even though she thought he was joking, Helen still felt a prick of jealousy at the possibility that Michael was admiring another woman. Being very careful of the degree of nonchalance she employed, in case Fergal should break the habit of a lifetime and be paying attention to the nuances of her voice, she said, 'You can't be serious. That girl has a mouth like a fertiliser sack.'

But Michael was serious. He went and spoke to the object of his new fixation during the band's break, and even managed to bring her back to where they were sitting, and introduced her. Neither Helen nor Fergal said much to her. Fergal assumed that their taciturnity was out of some sort of loyalty to Loretta. Helen was wondering whether or not it was a good idea to get drunk.

When the singing began again, Michael took the slip of paper on which she had written her name and looked at it, reverently, for a long time. When, at the end of the evening, they were pulling out of the car park, their headlights shone on the back of the Ploughboys' transit van. Kelly was standing there. Michael shouted, as if in panic, 'I have to say goodbye to her,' and jumped out of the car while it was still moving.

When they began to snog, still standing in the glare of the headlights, it was too much for Helen. She reached across and flicked the dimmer switch on and off.

Fergal laughed. 'Michael's a fast worker,' he said.

'I'm tired,' she said. 'I want to get home.'

All the way back from Kilbride, Helen went over the events at the Starlite Lounge fifteen days before, wondering at what point she could have intervened: whether she could have prevented it from happening. Michael had made her culpable, so culpable she must be. She was still muttering to herself when she parked outside her house and looked at the quiet tastefulness of it; the outward signs that it was the house of someone who was secure, mature and intelligent. She scanned the front of the house for clues as, in a similar frame of mind, one might scan one's face in the mirror.

'He never offered to fix my fucking windows,' she said.

Inside, the house was quiet. The children had been playing in the sitting room and had left their debris scattered across the floor. Irritably, automatically, she began to pick things up. She winced at her offspring's choice in playthings. There were the coy ponies with pink manes and the Steroid Avengers from the planet Grunt. There was Barbie and there was Ken. Barbie and Ken irritated her more than anything. Barbie looked complacent and Ken looked smug.

Holding Barbie in her left hand, Helen unhooked one of her earrings and straightened the hook so that it was like a long blunt pin. She was about to stick the pin in Barbie when she changed her mind and picked up Ken instead. She turned him over and thrust the pin in him, straight up his backside.

She had not noticed Fergal, slippershod, come into the room.

'What's the matter?' he asked. His expression bordered on the interested.

'Nothing,' she said. 'I'm tired. I need a holiday.'

∫

DOYLE'S CROSS

ʃ

For a great part of the journey out from Doyle's Cross to Peshawar, Eileen Patterson-Smythe (Cullen that was) was preoccupied with expectation. In 1936 you did not travel from County Wexford to the subcontinent of India for trivial or whimsical reasons. Nothing short of an entire change of life could justify the days of packing her trousseau under her mother's vicious eyes, and the embarrassment of her father's whiskey tears at parting, and the squalor of the packet to England, and a week of playing the poor relation to her new in-laws at Salisbury.

She should have realised that it was only sour grapes that made those Edwardian hens look down their narrow English noses at her, and mock her accent behind her back. She had married, had stolen, their brother, the only son and heir. She had deprived them of the sole male of their flock, the youngest member of their family, and for this castration they were paying her back in drops of venom. Iris, Violet and Lily: looking at their dry, tight mouths, Eileen couldn't help thinking how those names were wasted. When she had first heard talk of this triad she had formed a picture altogether different from the *memento mori* that sat with her in Cathedral Close, looking out across the lawn to where Charles was sitting in a deck chair, in white clothes and a straw hat.

'Charles looks simply dreadful these days.'

It didn't matter which of them had made the remark – she knew that it was directed at her. She studied her husband, and tried to remember what he had looked like when she first saw him, and tried to work out in what way he had deteriorated under her stewardship. She saw what she had always seen: the silhouette of a British Army Officer in mufti. He was doing nothing, and appeared to be thinking nothing and, what was more, he showed every sign of being contented in that state or, at least, of being accustomed to it. Eileen smiled at Iris, Violet and Lily, as though this latest barb had been a pleasantry, and as though their eyes were not going over her Dublin-made dress, stitch by stitch.

To begin with, the boredom of days at sea was a relief when compared with her stay at Salisbury, but, as her own conversation petered out, Charles's taciturnity became burdensome. She would begin to tell him things and, halfway through the sentence, remember that it was something she had told him before, and she would stop abruptly. Charles would nod at her in his vacant manner as if she had finished her story.

He would say, 'I say.'

She was beginning to think that I-say was her Christian name. He never called her Eileen, or Darling. In revenge she stopped calling him Charley, as she used to, and said Charles!, in a tone of voice that one of his sisters might have used. At first she did it as a joke, but when he seemed not to notice she kept it up until it became habitual.

'Charles!'

'I say.'

It was sunset on the Mediterranean and she was a new bride, three and a half weeks into her marriage. She wanted to laugh at the preposterousness of it, but she had heard the words mad and Irish too often in conjunction to want to fuel the stereotype with behaviour that would be irrational to her fellow passengers.

'Nothing. I was just wondering about India. You haven't really told me what it's like.'

He made a noise of satisfaction in his throat and, for a moment, his eyes became less vacant, as though the mention of India had conjured up a pleasant memory: of sticking pigs perhaps, or of long, silent evenings in the company of his brother-officers.

Knowing, by now, that that was as much of an answer as she could expect, she shuffled the cards that were in her hand and laid out another row of Patience. The cards had a picture of the Taj Mahal on the back. They were a going-away present from Caroline.

Caroline had been, if anything, more enthusiastic about the marriage than Eileen. 'You're lousy with luck Eileen Cullen. India! I'll be stuck here in the rain the rest of my life while you're out there in the hot sun surrounded with jewels and Maharajahs and tigers on leads like greyhounds.'

Eileen covered the Taj Mahal with the eight of clubs and was about to place a red seven on it when she heard a giggle and looked up to see two girls come round the corner, arm in arm. They were well dressed and about nineteen years of age, and a woman, who might have been their mother, walked four paces behind them. Eileen smiled at the girls, and they smiled back at her, but the mother was looking Charles over in a manner that could only be called speculative. Then her eyes fell on Eileen, and located the third finger of her left hand. At the sight of the small gleam of gold the woman's eyes glazed over and she produced a sigh of what might have been resignation. And she walked on in pursuit of her daughters.

Eileen detected, coming from Charles's direction, the grunt that he used to indicate amusement. 'I say,' he said. 'The Fishing Fleet.' He used the expression as though it was an original thing to say; as though he had had the wit to invent such a term.

Eileen laughed, and Charles beamed, minutely, to think

he had amused her. She was not, however, laughing at her husband's feat of eloquence, but at the pathos of a woman who felt it necessary to travel to India to find husbands for her daughters, a thing her own mother would have done readily had she the funds and imagination. And, Charles, when she met him, had originally come to Doyle's Cross on a fishing holiday. And, she had overheard her father describe Charles as a great catch. She laughed, most of all, as a way of releasing stored laughter.

She had difficulty sleeping at sea. The instability of the ship disturbed her dreams, and she woke often; more often as they headed south into the heat. When she woke, in the undulating dark, she remembered the faces and tones of Iris, Violet and Lily and, without knowing why she was doing it, she found herself practising their vowels and consonants aloud, to the accompaniment of Charles's breathing, and the hum of the ship's engines far below.

Sometimes, she wondered if she might stroke the hair of his thighs.

At Port Said Charles went ashore for an hour. She had declined to accompany him. She regretted her refusal ten minutes after he had gone, and walked the decks on the landward side of the ship, watching out for his return. She would have liked to think that this was on account of love, but it was not. She walked because it was so hot that when she sat still her back stuck to the deck chair. She looked out for him because in his company she had not made the acquaintance of any of the other passengers. She walked slowly, with her arms held slightly away from her sides, to prevent sweat from accumulating.

'Summer clothes me eye,' she thought, as she pulled the damp sleeve of her dress away from her arm. Caroline had gone with her to Dublin to help her choose, and everything they had bought was in the lightest material possible. Dresses you would freeze in on a summer's day in Doyle's Cross. Caroline had warned her that the heat would be unimaginable. She had read it in a novel. And Port Said was still a long way north of Bombay. Eileen couldn't see how she was going to live in these temperatures. She watched the men who squatted by the quay and allowed the flies to roam their bodies. She wondered if it was because they had dark skin and whether dark skin was less sensitive to the legs of a fly than pale skin. She longed to ask someone, but couldn't think of a way to phrase the question which didn't sound mildly obscene. She consoled herself that there would be plenty of dark-skinned people in India whom she could ask, once she had got to know them.

She began to worry that Charles would get lost in Port Said, and the ship sail without him.

At forty-two, Charles might have been considered a little old for her, but you can't have everything, supposedly. And Eileen, at twenty-three, had been getting to be a bit of an old maid herself. She hadn't fallen in love with him, but had fallen for him on the rebound, because he seemed kind, and harmless, and he had said something which had made her laugh at a time when she thought that she might never laugh again. It was odd, she thought, that there had been no evidence of this humorous side of him since.

As far as she was concerned it had been a diverting flirtation with a passing tourist, but as soon as she brought him through the door of the house and her mother set eyes on him it became a toboggan ride to the altar. They had married in the small church in Doyle's Cross within a month of meeting. The haste was justified because of Charles's need to return to India once his leave was up. There was a garrison, apparently, in need of his command. The rector, given a choice between a rushed wedding and unwashed hordes rushing over the Khyber Pass, allowed himself to be swayed in favour of the opinions of Eileen's mother, who was the sort of woman a rector didn't cross unless he had his sights set on another, distant, parish.

She walked the deck at Port Said, and mulled over the

idea of dinner parties. One of the few things Charles had told her was that, as the colonel's wife, she would be obliged to give dinners. She thought of black bejewelled guests, and punkahs causing eddies in the smoke trails of long cigarettes. These were scenes which Caroline had described to her when persuading her to accept Charles's proposal. These were advantages she could have as Mrs Charles Patterson-Smythe, which would have been unthinkable had she realised her original plan and become Mrs Christopher Connors.

She took extraordinary pleasure in imagining Christopher Connors turning up at her dinner table one of the days and sitting in starvation corner, watching her play the hostess from beneath his thick yellow eyebrows, longing and regret palpable on his face.

A voice at her shoulder said, 'I say.'

She turned to see Charles, who had come up the gang-plank without her noticing.

Although it was even hotter in Bombay than it had been in Port Said, she had, by some physiological quirk, adjusted to the heat by the time she went ashore, and the train journey to Delhi, which might have been unbearable, became an adventure of colour and excitement. Outside the window men in pink dhotis tended cows with gilded horns, and the earth rose in clouds of red dust in the wake of women swathed in silver thread and blue. Every station platform was a bedlam of commerce and mendicity. And, at Delhi, a young subaltern was more than polite to her when Charles left her alone on the platform for ten minutes. When he swept off his cap to her he had muscles which rippled across his forehead, which was something she noticed because half of his forehead was brown and half of it white – the white half surmounted with brown hair – so that he gave the impression of a walnut and cream cake she had once had in Waterford.

She moved her left hand slightly, so that the ring showed,

and he faded into the crowd. Other women would get off the train who would be better suited to his approaches.

The succession of trains and the endless days aboard them lulled her into a state of contentment. Whenever she saw something new out of the window she would point it out and call Charles's name, and he would explain it in two words or less, by naming it and, sometimes, adding an adjective.

'*Sadhu*,' he might say, and add, 'Rum chaps.'

By cobbling together his telegrammatic explanations with what she remembered of Caroline's fictions, Eileen began to form an idea of the country she was to live in. It wasn't until they reached a point about halfway between Lahore and Rawalpindi that something in the atmosphere made her feel uneasy. It was something so unexpected that, at first, she would not express her sensation for fear that she might have imagined it. Only when her teeth began to chatter was she compelled to mention it to Charles.

'Why is it cold? Aren't you cold?'

He looked at her, somewhat surprised, and, nodding in the direction of the window, said, 'Himalayas. Winter.'

They had started out at the end of an Irish summer and spent much of the autumn travelling, and now they were going north into a Himalayan winter. Eileen focused hard out of the window, expecting to make out snow-capped mountains in the distance.

'Himalayas?' she said. 'You never mentioned anything about the Himalayas. India, you said.'

She was saved from collapsing in tears by the incomprehension on his face, and by the necessity of explaining her predicament to him.

'I haven't a stitch,' she said. 'I brought all summer clothes. I thought we were going somewhere hot.'

At the mention of women's clothing Charles became speechless with embarrassment. It was not a subject which he had been prepared for by bachelor life on the North-West

Frontier. He stared at the toecaps of his shoes and waited to see if the problem would unravel itself, or whether he would have to think of a solution.

'I wasn't prepared for this,' she said.

'Ah,' he said. He knew the answer to that one. 'Time spent doing a reconnaissance,' he said.

'What?' she said.

'Is seldom time wasted,' he said.

That was when she did collapse in tears, and he realised that he had a situation on his hands. He ran through all the remedies for cold and emotional incontinence that were known to him until he thought of the appropriate solution. He pulled a small case down from the overhead rack and extracted a whiskey flask. He poured some of the liquid into the cap and offered it to his wife.

The whiskey proved to be an adequate solution in the short-term, but there came a moment when Eileen, although too inebriated to feel the cold to any great extent, started shivering in an alarming manner. Charles jumped off the train at the next station and returned within three minutes with a kind of coat, which was large and made of goatskin, which had not been cured to perfection.

He wrapped the coat around her, tenderly, she thought. He sat back in his seat to admire his handiwork. There was a bit of a stink, but Eileen looked more comfortable, and she slid into the corner and fell asleep. He took a small nip of the remaining whiskey in self-congratulation.

She was woken by a hand on her shoulder and her new name, I-say, being repeated over and over. She felt as though someone had inserted the spike of an umbrella through the back of her skull. Charles was beaming down at her, and she had never seen him smile so widely.

'We're here,' he said. 'And they've got the band out.'

Eileen Patterson-Smythe (Cullen no more) staggered off the train, reeking of goatskin and whiskey and wearing the coat of an Afghan shepherd. She was still drunk enough not to feel, to its full extent, the embarrassment that would creep over her later at the memory of this moment; the embarrassment which, to some extent, would dominate the rest of her life. On the platform the town and garrison dignitaries stood in rows to have their hands shaken and a full military band played 'Scotland the Brave' in honour of the colonel's new bride. At her side, supporting her by the elbow, for which she was grateful, Charles glowed with pleasure at being back among his own kind.

∫

THE ROWER

ſ

You take the road from New Ross to Kilkenny and cross the Barrow by Mount Garret Bridge, and turn right by the grey house on the corner as if you were going to Graiguenamanagh and, if you are not driving too fast, you will find yourself passing through The Rower, where you might notice the scattering of houses along the main road, but you will see no people. You will need to ask directions to find the house of Lily Stevens, so it is best to go into the shop, if it is open, and ask there. They will send you towards her by rough lanes and complicated turnings, and no matter how well you understand the directions you will be lost once or twice. Be prepared for reversing in narrow dead-ends, with your back wheels spinning in the heavy mud. There was one memorably wet winter when Lily Stevens' husband had to pull the harvester through the fields with a bulldozer to save the sugar-beet.

The house is almost square and covered with a lattice of dormant Virginia creeper. The front door faces a small garden surrounded by a low wall and intersected by neglected bushes of acrid box. In the damp air it is this smell of box which dominates the garden. The door is painted yellow, and has not been opened within the span of my memory. Drive into the yard at the back and let yourself in through the porch door, past the rusting, humming freezer and into the kitchen. You may find someone there to make yourself known to, and you might not. Lily Stevens' son and his family live in a bungalow they have built on the other side of the haggard.

There is not much time left. It has been known for some weeks now that Mrs Stevens is near death, and most of the people who would have done so have come to The Rower to take their leave of her. And prepare yourself. She is so far gone now that she may not recognise you, and you might find it disturbing to hear the noise she makes as she tries to breathe, small and lost in the middle of her bed. She doesn't really speak any more, because of the effort it takes to get the words from her brain to her mouth through the fug of painkillers. Her last words have yet to be recorded, but she has had her last conversation.

'Don't just stand there,' she said. 'Come and sit by me.'

There was no chair, so I made a place for myself among the newspapers and dictionaries and old Penguin paperbacks on the end of the bed, and sat on the pattern of small pink flowers that covered her quilt. Under my weight the bed groaned and the feathers made a sigh of compaction.

'I didn't think you'd know me,' I said.

A flicker of humour passed across her face. She had never been someone who tolerated false modesty and so, between us, a statement such as the one I had just made could only be taken as a joke. All the same, it was three years since I had last been home; since I had last seen her, and then we had only the briefest of conversations, in the middle of the street in New Ross. She was still sprightly then, young for her eighty years, still driving herself into town once a week to do her shopping. She had made me promise that I would come out to The Rower to see her before I went away again. I had broken my promise, and I still remember the guilt I felt as the plane flew south from Dublin, over the deadening cloudscape that passed for a view.

The bed creaked again with some small movement I made.

'You have a good colour,' she said. 'Are you still in the same place?'

'I've just moved to Lisbon. But the climate's the same.'

'Lisbon,' she said. She was silent for a few moments, not as though she had nothing to say, but more as though she was taking a little rest before continuing. I read the spines in the bookcases while I waited.

She said, 'I have a book of Portuguese poetry somewhere there. I can't remember the man's name, but I suppose you know it anyway. Not good, but very earnest.'

She looked over at her bookshelves, somewhat helplessly.

I said, 'It tends to be a bit like that. I think the Portuguese have been brutal for so long that, since the revolution, they have found that there is nothing left in them but goodness and earnestness.'

'It sounds very dull,' she said.

'It would be,' I said, 'if it was true.'

She began to laugh at that, but the pain that was brought upon her at the beginnings of laughter was so great that it defeated her amusement.

After a while I read the clues of the *Irish Times* crossword to her and wrote in the answers she gave. The crosswords of the previous few days were on the bed, each one filled in by the hand of a different visitor.

'You haven't married yet?' she said.

'No.'

'I never thought you would.'

There was no need to give her more information. From my one word of denial she had divined more than I could divulge.

I was nine years old when I first came into her sphere of influence. She was my schoolteacher for two years. I can't remember any lesson that she taught me, but I can remember having conversations with her in the classroom;

talking with her as though the two of us were alone and the thirty other children around me had faded into the gloss-painted walls. I can remember the day I handed her an essay and, after she had read it, she sent one of the children next door to fetch Sister Philomena. Sister Philomena was head of the school, and our days were punctuated by the screaming which came through the glass and wood folding partition between her classroom and ours. The children under this nun's care had a cowed look about them, and scarlet palms where she had beat them with her leather. Because of the noise from next door, we were aware, every day, of the good fortune we had to be taught by Mrs Stevens, whose voice was seldom raised and whose hand never came down on one of ours in anger.

The messenger returned, followed by Sister Philomena. At the sight of the nun, clutching her leather in the pocket of her apron, my flesh turned to molten tar. The nun scanned the classroom and rested her eyes on me, knowing, by my terror, that I was the one for whom she had been called. She drew her leather out as she addressed Mrs Stevens in harsh Irish.

I tried to review all the words I had put in the essay, to know where I had transgressed. I couldn't think what sin I had committed that was so grave it had made Mrs Stevens summon the head: a thing she had never had cause to do before. My eyes were fixed on the leather, an instrument known to all schoolchildren of the time, since it had been invented and manufactured for their punishment and no other reason. Sister Philomena had refined hers by splitting it down the centre for half its length, doubling the pain it could inflict.

We were standing as the nun entered, out of respect, as we were obliged to do. As Mrs Stevens handed her my essay we were commanded to sit down. My legs were too weak to sit down in a controlled way, and I hit the seat with a thud. That was when I looked at Mrs Stevens and saw that she was smiling at me.

After the reading Sister Philomena and Mrs Stevens had a short discussion. Since they were speaking Irish, as teachers were supposed to when in front of their pupils, I could only understand one word in ten, but I caught enough of it to know that it was complimentary and that it concerned me. Then the nun bid us good morning and we all rose to our feet again and, just before she swept out of the room, she gave me a big, condescending smile.

Years later, I asked Lily why she had shown the nun that essay. It was after Lily had retired and after I had left school; in the days when I used to cycle out to The Rower to spend the afternoon with her on Sundays, drinking tea and talking about poetry.

Lily said, 'I had to show her how intelligent you were. I knew, if I did that, she would never allow you in her own class. She didn't like pupils who might be a match for her. I didn't want her to be beating the spirit out of you.'

Before Lily had told me that, I had always assumed, in all the class and teacher permutations of my time at school, that it was luck that had kept me away from Sister Philomena and the lick of her leather.

Lily Stevens was the daughter of two schoolteachers, and her mother's parents were both schoolteachers before that. They had all spent their whole lives teaching in the same school in the same town. So that, for many years, it was said that there was no native of New Ross who had not come under the tutelage of one of that family. Lily had broken with tradition by marrying a farmer, and, since none of her children had shown any interest in becoming a teacher, she was, in some respects, the last of her line.

On her bookshelves there was a first edition of *Ulysses* which Joyce had sent to her mother. The parish priest of the time had come to hear of the existence of the book and instructed Lily's mother to burn it. To save a scandal the book had to be hidden, and to be read in secret. Lily's father was an amateur Greek scholar who had made his own translation of Pindar. This also had to be kept a secret from the town, since it was that part of the *Pythian Odes* which rejected immortality in favour of possibility. They had less clandestine possessions too, letters to various family members from Yeats and Synge and Mahaffy, which were reduced to tattered shreds by being read and re-read.

There were times in the life of the town when Lily's family seemed to be the only thread of life running through the place. Times when the state was young and, for want of an identity, De Valera was allowed to impose his ideal of the Irish as an innocent peasantry, by repression and censorship; times when the thugs of the Old IRA were allowed to swagger unchallenged, before the Provisionals made that acronym shameful. There were others, of course, with the courage to think for themselves, but, by and large, they went away: to fight in Spain, to live in Russia, to labour in North London, to teach Portuguese schoolchildren the English language in my own case. It was Lily's family who stayed behind and kept the thin-spun thread of the intellect running through our town. Perhaps there were others, but that is the family I know of.

'I failed with you,' she said. She said this to me as she lay on her deathbed, after she had finished the crossword, after I had said twice that I must be tiring her, that I should be going.

'I failed with you. I wanted you to become a writer, not a teacher.'

'That's my own fault, not yours.'

The look she gave me was sceptical. She knew and I knew. It was because of knowing her that I had come to consider teaching to be the higher calling of the two. Perhaps if I had been beaten by Sister Philomena, that might have made a writer of me; a solitary introspective, each thuck of the typewriter keys a blow of the leather returned to the nun.

I tried to justify myself. 'There are too many mediocre writers and not enough good teachers. Hardly any good teachers at all.'

'Good or bad you might be,' she said. 'Mediocrity isn't in you.'

She said that she wanted her pills, and gave me instructions, and I took a pill from each of five bottles on her bedside table, and held her head, and gave them to her in the right order, one by one, with a sip of water between each. The back of her head was soft and light. I realised that, in all the years I had known her, it was the first time I had touched her. I thought of all the lovers I had touched more intimately who had not known me so well.

After the pills, after I had replaced her head on the pillow as if it were an unconnected object, she closed her eyes, and I wondered if she had gone to sleep. I waited some minutes, standing by her head, thinking that I should go and leave her to rest. I knew that this was our last conversation, and that was why I hesitated. I moved my feet.

'No,' she said. 'Don't go. I'm not finished.'

I sat again on the tracery of pink flowers and the bed groaned again under my weight. She smiled.

Without opening her eyes, she said, 'You're getting to the age when you should be minding your weight. Wait till you're like me and you have your work cut out keeping an ounce of flesh about you.'

'Fat chance,' I said.

She opened her eyes.

It must have been the drugs. When she opened her eyes there was an urgency and a vitality in them.

'You're back,' I said.

'I'm back.'

She said, 'Did you notice my Agave, on the windowsill?'

'Yes?' I said.

Although I hadn't noticed the plant before, I had turned around as she spoke, and seen it. It was a spiny star in a pot, eighteen inches across and like any other Agave on a windowsill.

She said, 'You wouldn't think it was twenty years old. I brought it back from Portugal when it was a tiny offshoot. If I'd left it where it was it would be seven feet wide by now. It might have flowered and died this summer. I was only in Portugal the once and the thing I loved most was the sight of the flowering Agaves. Monocarpic, is that what you call it? They wait and they grow and when they are ready they throw a flower twenty feet into the sky. And then, of course, they die. What else could they do? But this one; this unfortunate on the windowsill; this one can only get older and older until it dies of oldness. This is the wrong climate for flowering.'

The thing I said next, the answer I gave, was said with a streak of cruelty in it, with a streak of truth in it.

I said, 'It isn't a question of climate. It is a question of treatment. Physiology is applicable, even in The Rower.'

And her answer was, 'I knew you wouldn't fail me.'

She said, 'I am going to die, and I am not going to die without saying this to someone, and it is just as well you are here because, of the people I know who are still living, you are the best person I can tell it to. And don't flatter yourself: it is only because I know you are someone who will write it down. Things must be written down. If Pindar had never written it down, a thousand people might have thought the same thing since and not known that they had thought it, because they couldn't express themselves so well. You might consider yourself Jungian, but only because Jung wrote it down instead of keeping it to himself. There, you have the greatest contradiction imaginable. If he had such faith in the collective mind, why did he need to tell anyone what he thought? Never mind. The only thing I have to tell you, after eighty-three years, after teaching thousands of children to read and write, after reading Shakespeare and Yeats to rows of children's heads, after teaching my own children to use the lavatory and hold their knives in their right hands and their forks in their left, after loving one man exclusively from his youth to his death; the only thing I have to tell you is something you know already and haven't realised. I'm offering you a short cut so that you can know this now and not wait, like me, until you are a skeleton on your deathbed. The only thing I have to tell you is that almost everyone you will ever meet on this green earth is someone who has spent their whole life with their head stuffed up their backside.'

Having said this, she left a gap for my astonishment and looked at me with drug-wide opened eyes, challenging me to contradict her. I said nothing.

'Head-in-the-arse is the human condition,' she said, as though a vulgarisation of her philosophy would penetrate further.

I said nothing.

She closed her eyes for four minutes, and when she opened them again she said, 'I know what you are thinking. This is an easy thing to say. Anyone could come to the same conclusion after a casual observation of the human race. You can talk to almost anyone and conclude that the only thing they have ever seen is the inside of their own colon. With your modern mind you are thinking that it is the fault of their nurturing; that every human is an extraordinary creation who could be a Mozart or a Sophocles if they hadn't been irreparably damaged by their upbringing. Once upon a time I thought the same thing. I lived by the same creed. I became a teacher, not because my parents were teachers, but because I thought I could draw the Prometheus out of every child, without liver damage. It was when I had my own children that I realised I had been wrong. I loved them and I taught them and they grew up with their heads stuffed up their arses. And then I began to have pupils like you. You weren't the only one. You came to me from stupid parents, but still you had the intelligence to see the world around you. Before I ever met you. Before I had the chance to draw it out of you, you knew it already. I kept you from Sister Philomena so that you could write things down. If your only reason for not writing it down is your fear of mediocrity then I have failed you. And the thing that damns you to hell is that you have failed yourself.'

When she had said all this her eyes closed again, but this time it was unconsciousness which closed them. I waited, to be sure that she had nothing more to say. Dusk fell in the room. Her daughter-in-law came to see to her needs, and I left.

There is still time. You can still go to The Rower and take your leave of her, but she has had her last conversation. She has exhausted the realm of the possible. And I have written it down.

∫

SLADE

$\int$

We had lived on peaches alone in Monte Carlo, and slept on half the beaches in the northern half of the Mediterranean; had outstayed our welcome in the houses of Italians and watched a naked, muscular Dutchman, with dreadlocks halfway down his glistening black back, play Macbeth in a scaffolding castle on the polder. We played it gay and straight, depending on whom we didn't want to sleep with, for Emma was saving herself for a romantically thin man at Manchester University, and I was just saving myself.

She thought she was in love, and wanted to find out, because her greatest fear was that it would never happen to her, and so I knew, as soon as the novelty of being a Eurobum had worn off, that she would want to go to Manchester. And, Manchester not being a place I had ever dreamed of seeing, we said goodbye on the Lüneburg Heideland, and I looked for an autobahn, to go south again.

I hadn't yet found out that fate is never to be trusted, so when the man in the first car that stopped for me said that he was going to the same town as I was, the very next street indeed, I took it for an omen: a good omen, naturally. He was studying to be a theologian and we passed the long, concrete-hemmed hours with talk of biblical prohibitions, among other things. Had I not been seventeen, and had he not been so polite, a subtext might have floated nearer the surface of our conversation.

In a moment of courage I told him that I was going to Heilbron for love, not simple friendship. I said that I had never been there before and asked him what it was like.

He said that I would soon find out.

The street where he dropped me was badly lit, with railway tracks on one side and small factories down the other. There was only one house. It was a solid, forbidding house, the strength of its presence barely mitigated by the single cherry tree that passed for a front garden. What had been the back garden was now the gherkin pickling factory, and the dormitories for the workers. Frau Jater, the owner, lived in the house still, with her cowed small husband and supercilious children, close to the stench of her own vinegar.

This cherry tree, it transpired, was something of a totem to the Jaters. Old hands, who were spending their second summer in the factory, said that the Jaters venerated the thing as though it were more precious than the house itself, and at cherry time they guarded it, night and day, from phantasmic marauders. They little knew that the real marauders had no designs on the fruit, but were plotting against the tree itself.

It was Jimmy Sullivan who was the leader of the hate campaign against the tree. He would lie on his bunk in the evenings, fantasising aloud, rambling on ways to kill or maim a cherry tree: axes and petrol and poison pellets drilled deep into the bole. His eyes would narrow and his breathing shallow, as if his secret kink might be dendrocide. He had determined that, on his last day, he would do something, and have his revenge on Frau Jater by harming the thing she loved most. I didn't understand why he hated the woman so much. I had yet to meet her.

I knew of a foolproof, failsafe, undetectable way to commit the crime, but I wasn't saying anything. I had a soft spot for cherry trees, and Jimmy Sullivan's talk made me think, protectively, of the cherry tree at home in Slade; the Morello crouched in the lee of a stone north wall that separated it from the sea and the salt-laden gales. The Morello never did well and my mother often said, as she stretched the fruit to a second pot of jam, that the salt was to blame, and that it wasn't the only thing in her garden that was sickened on account of it.

Since Donald was the only reason I had come to that place, I'd watch him to see if he was more in favour of the tree or against the Jaters, but he had other problems that summer, and was even more disconnected than his usual, ethereal self. Because there wasn't a bed spare, and because I wasn't supposed to be there at all, I slept in the same bed as him, which was how I would have slept for preference in any case. We assumed that it was assumed that we were lovers. And that was fine, because it was part of the elaborate double bluff we played on ourselves. If we didn't mind whether people thought we were poofs that just showed how secure we were in our heterosexuality – at least, how secure Donald was in his heterosexuality, for he was the one person who knew the full extent of my experiments, by which I tried to provoke him into jealousy, or disgust, or passion, or something other than the graciousness of his all-forgiving smile. At Heilbron the smile was less evident, but then, so was he.

Everything stank of vinegar, all the time. There were some who had given up washing themselves and their clothes, as a waste of time, just waiting it out until they were back in the suburban bathrooms of Bray. We had no great need to keep our dignity intact, unlike the Turkish men and the Italian women in the other dormitories, for whom this was life. For us, it was an unpleasant but interesting episode; a way to stretch a grant. We were suffering now to buy beer money for the winter, not to feed a family at home in the hills.

I say we, meaning they. My motives for being in that place were not clear to me. Except that when I had nothing better to do I always chose to be as close to him as possible. I tried to get a job in the factory to begin with, and after that I just hung around, performing little domestic services for Donald to pass the time while he worked, and sat in the town square in the sunshine with an old tramp from Transylvania who, indeed, had overdeveloped canine teeth and the sort of hatchet face you'd associate with a B-movie vampire. He pushed all his possessions before him in a shopping trolley and his feet were mummified in layers of bags and rags. Every day, at the same time, he would spend an hour and a half unwrapping these feet, to wash them in the fountain, before settling to his lunch of sausage. He was a chatty soul, but our conversation was limited because he had worked once on an American airbase, and the only words in English he knew were FuckinGoddam sonofabitch. I wondered sometimes what one had to do to become like him. But, in the end, I decided that I didn't have the bone structure.

I can't remember now what caused the strike. There is a vague recollection that Donald was at the centre of it, but that may be a pathetic, retrospective wish on my part to inflate the importance he had to the world in general. In any case, I'm sure it happened on the day I was sent shoplifting.

'Oh, and nick some cheese, while you're there.'

He threw the instruction at me casually, at the end of a list of things I was to buy in the supermarket. Shoplifting, for the rest of them, was no big deal. The theory was that the Germans were so honest that they suspected nothing. One Northsider had achieved glory by filling a trolley with food and putting a crate of beer on the shelf at the bottom and wheeling the whole thing out of the back door of the shop and all the way home. I had been with Donald when he nicked things. I knew the system: you put the object of your illicit desires on that folding, child-seat thing and, when no one was looking, you knocked it from there into your pocket.

I was an hour in that small supermarket, wheeling that bloody thing up and down the three short aisles, sweating like a racehorse and staring at that obnoxious yellow lump, before I finally had the courage to pocket it and rush to the checkout. The girl in the pale pink overall should have thought I was a madman, but she didn't have the imagination.

All the way back I shook like a greyhound, knowing now what I had long suspected – that I wasn't cut out for crime. At that stage deciding on a career was still a process of elimination. I knew well enough what I wanted to do. I just hadn't worked out a system which combined doing it with eating the odd meal. I tended to be good at the sort of things which were, unfortunately, their own reward. If you could make money by being in love I would have been a tycoon, even at that age.

I waited in the dormitory for the lads to come in for their break. It was that time of day when the sun fell across the bottom of a bed by one of the windows and I lay, with my face in the light, thinking of things to say to Donald. I wanted to tell him never to ask me to steal again, but couldn't work out how to say it without making it obvious that I would have done whatever he asked. In my mind, a balance had to be maintained, lest he should think that I loved him more than he me. Only in my mind for, in retrospect, it was obvious to anyone which of us was tying himself in knots of love.

They came in whooping like revolutionaries. There had been an altercation and someone had called out 'strike', and the whole of the Irish had walked out in a body. Production had been stopped for ten minutes, the Germans had panicked and the lads had won. They were snowed with their success; muscles charged and pupils dilated and the endless, fascinated repetition of the details. It was, in some respects, the first victory in the war against the Jaters.

Hostilities were engaged with whatever weapons came to hand: whoever was on cleaning duty would empty the sweepings into the gherkin vats; whoever was packing the jars into boxes would unscrew each lid a little; whoever had a spanner in their hand would drop it in the works. I suppose, symbolically, hiding me in the dormitory became part of the defiance. Frau Jater took to making surprise visits at odd hours, but we had our lines of defence. The man nearest the door would take his shorts off and stand there naked, which gave me time to jump into a cupboard or under a bed. It got to the stage where I seemed to be staying in the place as a matter of principle.

The night she came round with the police we had plenty of warning from the floor below, and Donald grabbed me by the sleeve and dragged me into the lavatory. While the policemen hammered on the door he pretended to be having faecal difficulties and I jumped out of the window into the arms of Jimmy Sullivan and Con Crowley and sped across the road and the railway tracks, my exit covered, as in all the most thrilling chases, by a hurtling train. What we didn't know was that the police were after an armed robber and if they'd seen me running like that I might have been in real trouble. All good *Boy's Own* stuff, I suppose.

That weekend we went sunbathing in the hills, by the edge of a wood overlooking vineyards, and talked about why vineyards were so ugly, and talked about tumescence, in an academic way, as if that were not the reason I was lying on my stomach to talk about it, and came back down through the steep woods, with that feeling of light-headed satisfaction you get from sunbathing and descent.

He asked me if I had called home yet, and I said that I hadn't. The mention of home, even in the deep, green shadows of that Germanic wood, made me think of the paleness of the light at Slade and the cold, solid colours in the sea and the brittle paleness of the rocks, and details: the plumes of rhubarb flower in the garden and the dead smell of crisp seaweed.

'You'll have to find out,' he said. 'Sooner or later.'

'Will I?'

Finding out was not part of the plan I had in mind. It seemed as good a time as any to let him in on the future I had decided for us.

'We don't have to go back. Neither of us. Why should we? There's nothing left for us there, apart from other people's expectations. For all you know Kay will decide to keep the child and you'll be blackmailed into marrying her. So, you go back – your life is over. If we go on the possibilities are endless.'

I looked at him, trying to gauge his reaction. His face had hardened to a carapace. The steepness of the path was sending small shocks through us with every step. Among the trees, small huts in fenced-off gardens had begun to appear; with coy, tasselled curtains at the windows and winsome garden furniture on the lawns.

'I've decided,' I said. 'I can't go back.'

'Fuck,' he said.

'What?'

He grabbed my elbow and shoulder and pushed me behind a stand of trees.

'The Jaters,' he said. 'I don't think they saw us.'

The Jaters were eating, in the afternoon sunshine, both of them wearing bathing costumes, like Mrs Sprat and Jack undressed. They sat on cushions on plastic chairs and a cloth of purple chenille covered the table. I couldn't help wondering what real harm there could be in people with such a penchant for kitsch.

Donald was hissing like a cat in a corner.

If Donald called home that evening it may well have been that he just wanted to talk to his family; it might not have been the act of betrayal that I took it for at the time. He came back from the phone box down the street, looking grave, looking as though he could have done without having to tell me what he was about to say. For the first time I became aware that I had become a problem to him, on top of everything else: I, who used to be his twin in hedonism. Being made to feel as callow as I did then would be enough to make anyone angry.

I remember he was standing in front of a poster of a dark haired girl, her legs spread in the usual, knickerless pose. Someone, perhaps it was me, had given her one of those speech bubbles we used to nick from public telephones, saying, *Ruf doch mal an.*

'They want to get in touch with you. They know you're here and the message is to phone. It's urgent.'

I was supposed to ask how urgent. I was supposed to hold my head despairingly, say 'Oh my God!' as in the most heart-wrenching dramas. Instead, I was wondering how much further I'd have to go before they wouldn't be able to get a message to me; to tell me news I knew already.

I wouldn't look at him.

'Apparently,' I heard him say, 'if you left now you'd make it for the funeral.'

I was aware, but only just, as though it were happening at a great distance, that he had put his hand on my forearm.

He had been talking softly, out of earshot of the others, who were getting ready to go out drinking for the night. At that, bludgeoned, moment the Frau Jater alarm sounded in the corridor, and Eoin Harvey stripped naked and I, automatically, took a dive beneath the bed we were sitting on.

She came in, backed by two Turks, and announced that they were taking a bed away, ignoring the nudity of Eoin Harvey and the tumult of protests from the lads that there wasn't a bed spare. There was, because someone had left for home that day, and she knew it. Still, with fifteen beds in the room, the chances of her directing her cohorts to remove my hiding place were slim. She looked as surprised as I did when the mattress was removed and we found ourselves staring at each other through the bedsprings. Her astonishment gave me just enough time to leap to my feet and my dignity.

Seldom has screaming felt so good. When I got to the bit about who won the fucking war anyway I was on a roll. Quick as a flash and beyond computation in decibels she reminded me that I was Irish, which opportunity I took to inform her that Irishness had not prevented half my family from joining the British Army for the sole purpose of slaughtering Nazi scum like her. Although, in the first moment of making her acquaintance, I had learned to hate her with all the force that I had failed to comprehend in Jimmy Sullivan, looking back across the years now I would like to think that she enjoyed our exchange as much as I did – but I doubt it. Though I hated her, she despised me, and there is no pleasure in despising.

When Frau Jater had gone and the lads had gone and we had arranged to join them later, I found myself clinging to the small of Donald's back, as he sat on his bed in the near-dark; as my body pumped out of itself a noisy, wet grief that I wanted no part of. Why should I have had to grieve for her when I never wanted her dead in the first place?

Jimmy Sullivan came back for something he had forgotten, and must have mistaken what we were doing for something just as private, and apologised for interrupting. I called him back and he stood in the half-lit door, uncertain.

'Salt,' I said, wiping the back of my salted face on Donald's shirt. 'You can kill the tree with a strong solution of salt, and no one will be the wiser.'

∫

RINGSEND

∫

Stanley waded out of the sea, calf deep, and the water threw patterns of reflection on his bare legs. He had, he considered, rather good knees. Other parts of him were flawed – his hands too narrow and tapering, his nose amorphous, his feet marred by tufts of hair – but his knees were a source of constant satisfaction to him. They were round and flat like the knees of horses he remembered from the time when there were horses. He came out of the water, dripping and cold, and dressed on the high tide mark. Because the morning was already hot, he wondered, not for the first time, why he felt compelled to wear clothes at all these days. He knew that he would feel silly walking naked through the empty streets, but there was something more than that: with all the clothes in the world at his disposal it might be wrong of him not to use them. A sin, perhaps, to waste them.

That speculation made him remember that he was running low on socks. He decided to make a detour through Grafton Street on his way home. He liked the excuse to go shopping, but had to discipline himself. In the beginning the freedom had gone to his head and he had collected so much clutter, and his house had become so full of everything that had taken his fancy, that he had been forced to move next door and use his own house as a sort of Museum of Materialism. These days he went through the shops trying to take only what he could persuade himself he needed.

His bicycle ride from the beach to the city centre took him through the suburbs, and then the streets, of North Dublin: pedalling fast where the roads were clear; swerving and weaving in other places, where cars had been abandoned all that time ago. Was it three, or was was it four years? He had meant to keep a record of the passing time, like Robinson Crusoe, but had soon given it up. Time, now that he was the only guardian of it, was counted not in months but in phases of depression and anxiety, which were fewer and fewer as time went on, and bouts of giddy happiness, which were constant, and states of complacent normality, such as now. He had been a little astonished that loneliness was not an emotion he suffered from. He had read a book about repression once and that had given him cause for anxiety, until he had considered his circumstances and decided that it would be pragmatic to leave loneliness repressed for the time being, if repressed it was.

He left the bicycle propped outside Browne Thomas and pushed through the doors. It was lucky, he supposed, that the cataclysm, or whatever it was, had occurred on a Tuesday morning when all the shops had been open, so that they had been left open in perpetuity for him. He would not have felt quite the same about his shopping trips had he been obliged to smash windows or crowbar shutters before every acquisition, perhaps setting off burglar alarms and wrecking the perfect silence of the city. He treasured that silence, broken only by the clicking of his bicycle wheels and the sound of breath leaving his body.

He made his way between dusty counters to the menswear department, where he chose a dozen pairs of socks in thin black silk. He liked the sort of socks that were so fragile and expensive that they could be worn only for a day and then thrown out, just as he liked the sort of shoes that were so expensive they lasted for ever. Not that a word like expensive had any currency any more, though it was hard for him to think of another to replace it. He wrapped the socks in tissue paper and put them in a bag. Before he left he wiped the dust from a couple of mirrors and tried on the cashmere jacket which he had been considering for some months. He studied himself with lips pursed for a few minutes before deciding that it did not really suit him. And, anyway, there was plenty of time to change his mind before autumn and the cold weather.

Leaving the shop, swinging his carrier bag between the perfume counters, he thought he heard a noise. A faint rustle perhaps, but certainly a noise of organic origin. He stopped, stiff in his tracks. Such a noise was not possible. He wanted to turn and look, but couldn't. Fear had frozen every muscle in his body. He was too frightened to shake, but could feel a sensation in his jaw as though his teeth were about to chatter.

Then a voice, emphatic with surprise and delight, said, 'Stanley Baldwin.'

It was a girl's voice, from somewhere on his right, behind the stack of moisturising lotions and the scratch'n'sniff display. He closed his eyes, and it crossed his mind that madness had crept upon him, and that the voice had its source in his insanity and not in reality. He was interested to notice that, of the possible explanations for the voice, his preference was madness. But he could hear footsteps, and the voice again.

'I thought it was you. Of all the people.'

Of all the people indeed. He recognised the voice. There could be no mistaking it and, of all the people left living, it would be Miriam Burke. Her voice was scored into his brain since the day he had first met her. It had been in the radiotherapy room of the Mater, in the days when the desperation of cancer had led him to believe that he should have one, final, attempt at a relationship with a woman. It was partly his experience of Miriam Burke which had sown the seeds of misanthropy in him, and left him one of the few people who might enjoy being, as he had believed he was, the last inhabitant of the planet.

His first practical thought, once he had accepted that the voice behind him was real, and that it was hers, was the calculation that he couldn't be sent to prison for her murder. The comfort of that allowed him to force a smile, open his eyes and turn towards her.

'Well,' he said.

'Well indeed,' she said. 'You're just in time. You can help me with this for a start. I was just trying it on when I heard you.'

She was wearing a short black dress of cut velvet and she turned her back to show that the zip was undone. She wriggled slightly as he pulled the mechanism upwards, over her bare, suntanned back.

'What do you think?' she asked, doing a twirl for him.

'A bit old-fashioned,' he said. 'I haven't seen anyone wear one of those for years.'

She laughed and poked him in the ribs. 'You were always a smart-alec.'

They stood for several minutes with nothing to say. She, not knowing whether to laugh or cry; he, fighting an instinct to leg it and get far from her until he had time to consider the implications of not having Dublin all to himself; both of them having mislaid what conversational skills they had, with the years of silence.

A folk memory stirred in his brain, and he said, 'D'you feel like a gargle?'

'Davy Byrne's?' she said.

'No. That place was always full of yuppies. I like The Parliament.'

In the pub he put himself behind the bar to pour the drinks, and stayed there for safety while she perched on a stool the other side of the counter. He made her some kind of blue and green cocktail, following her instructions, but refused to search for a paper umbrella to decorate it.

'Girls are so camp,' he said, with some derision.

'What?'

'Nothing.'

He pulled a pint of Guinness for himself.

'The last barrel,' he said. 'I have the place nearly drunk dry. I already ran through what was in The George before I came on to this place.'

She made no response, and he wondered if what he had said had sounded like boasting. Perhaps she was sulking about the paper umbrella. She was making him feel awkward and, at the same time, that she was gaining power over him, which he resented.

He said, 'It's a bit of a coincidence, isn't it? The two of us being the only ones left and knowing each other.'

'Not at all,' she said, 'I knew everyone.'

'I suppose,' he said.

'So,' she said, 'where were you when it happened?'

They told each other their stories of the Tuesday morning. He had been in the Mater having his radiation treatment. They had strapped him into the machine as usual, but instead of coming back for him after a few minutes they had left him for what seemed like hours, until he thought he was going to fry and had to get himself out of it. And then there was no one. Every living creature in the world had turned to vapour. As for the cancer, there had been no sign of that since. And she had more or less the same story, except that it had happened to her in a London hospital, and she had spent the years between in England, driving from one empty city to another until she finally took the risk and crossed the Irish Sea to find out if there was anyone left at home.

'Lucky I knew how to handle a boat,' she said.

'Yes,' he said, wondering whether she would notice the tone of regret in his voice.

'Do you think,' she asked, 'it was a war, or what? I didn't see anything about it in the papers that day.'

Her question produced symptoms of discomfort in him.

He said, 'I used to worry about that. I started to read what I could about the weapons and that. But there didn't seem much point in the end. Whatever it was, it was fairly conclusive.'

'Do you think it was fate?' she asked. 'Just the two of us left in the world?'

He squirmed with uneasiness.

'How do you mean?'

She reached a hand across to where his lay on the counter, and he flinched and drew back.

'Like Adam and Eve,' she said. 'It's up to us to get the whole thing going again.'

Her directness gave him the courage to defy her. He looked at her coldly, and said, 'You're taking a lot for granted.'

'What?'

'Paradise ended when Adam and Eve started that sort of hanky-panky.'

He said it with such deadly earnestness that she assumed, naturally, that he was joking. She laughed, loudly.

'You're deadly, Stanley Baldwin, so you are. Still the same.'

He let it drop at that, for the moment. Never having spelt it out in his previous life, he was disinclined to allow a creature like Miriam Burke to be the first to hear him say it. He had hoped that, by bringing her to this pub with its homoerotic posters and long established reputation, she would get the message of her own accord. From the way she was gazing at him and sucking on her swizzle stick it was obvious that a little bluntness might be called for. He pulled another pint for himself, while reviewing in his mind some of the less messy forms of murder: just in case.

She told him that she had moved into the Shelbourne,

and that she wanted to see where he lived. After a lot of persuasion he agreed to take her out to his house in Ringsend.

'Ringsend?' she said. 'What are you living out there for when you could have any house in Dublin? What's wrong with Merrion Square?'

'I like the sea,' he said. 'Anyway, Merrion Square is all banks.'

'Not any more it isn't,' she said.

Her second disappointment was that he travelled by bicycle. 'What do you have that yoke for when you could be driving any car in Dublin?'

He shrugged his shoulders and could think of nothing he wanted to say, but wheeled the bicycle between the two of them, down College Green, while she talked about the Trinity Balls of long ago.

Dublin, which had been such a comfort to him while it was empty, seemed eerie in her presence. The doubling of footfalls and the sound of her voice echoed too loud, drowning out the click of bicycle spokes that was normally his only companion. He thought of leaping onto the saddle and pedalling away up Nassau Street, but what then? He couldn't spend the rest of his life hiding from her. And how could he deny her a bit of company, when she had been craving it for so long; craving it probably as much as he had been enjoying the silence.

'Offer it up,' his granny would have said. He offered it up, for the moment.

He hated her coming into his house and looking at his things, and he winced every time she touched something. He finally shouted at her when she put her arms around his neck and tried to kiss him.

'No,' he yelled, pushing her away. 'I thought I told you. I don't want any of that.'

'Oh come on,' she said. 'What's the matter?'

'Nothing's the matter. Or nothing was the matter until you came along.'

'I don't understand you,' she said. 'You told me at Sally Dawes' twenty-first that I was the girl of your dreams.'

'And you laughed at me and ran off with some rugby-playing ape from Killiney.'

'Oh,' she said. 'I see. Playing hard to get now, to punish me.'

'No,' he said, and then, his head averted, he mumbled, 'Anyway, I'm gay.'

'What?'

'Gay,' he shouted. 'G-A-Y: queer.'

'Don't be stupid,' she said. 'You can't be gay. There aren't any men left. Anyway, you never were before. You were all over me at Sally Dawes'. And Finnoula Robinson did it with you. I know 'cause she told me.'

'Well I am now,' he screamed. Then, more calmly, he said, 'The thing with Finnoula Robinson was a disaster. I was only covering up for what was going on between her brother and me. You've no idea what it was like in those days.'

'Henry?' she said. 'My Henry? Henry Robinson? But we were practically engaged. Sweet Jesus.'

'Look,' he said. 'It doesn't matter now, does it? What can I say to you? For three years I've been in love with someone who happens to be a man; who happens to be myself, and I've been perfectly happy. As far as I'm concerned that makes me gay, no matter who or what I shagged in the old days. I don't want to start the human race all over again. I like things the way they are.'

'Ssh,' she said. 'Don't talk. You're upset.'

She pulled him down on the sofa beside her and put her arms around him and he, unresisting, allowed himself to be comforted.

'I'm sorry I can't be what you want,' he said. 'If you're staying around anyway, I suppose we could just be friends.'

She wasn't paying attention. She was looking out through

the back window. 'What kind of tree is that in the yard?' she asked.

He looked up. 'An apple tree, I think.'

'There'll be fruit in the autumn, so.'

She was thinking about the children they would have, once he had overcome his present, illogical way of looking at things. She wondered if history would repeat itself, and whether her first-born son would murder her second.

'You're out of luck there,' he said. 'There are no insects left to pollinate the flowers. Fruit is off the menu: forbidden or otherwise.'

∫

LEGACY

5

The money came through on Friday, seven months after
it was expected. Reasons for the delay had been given to
him all along and, towards the end, reasons had regressed
until, in Virgil's ears, they were spoken with the thin sound
of excuses. But you cannot expect a solicitor to defend
himself by declaring his own incompetence, and he had
tied Virgil's cause to himself by promises made from one
week to another; by spinning a thread of hope so ingenious
that you could not help but feel he was a clever man. It was
only afterwards that Virgil came to the just conclusion that,
had the solicitor used in the cause of the legacy one tenth
of the energy he had expended in dissimulation, the matter
could have been cleared up by early summer.

God, Virgil told himself, moves in mysterious ways. He
told himself this small and hackneyed truth; this get-out
clause of put-upon believers, as though it had the pro-
fundity of an original revelation. The phrase was one of
his greatest comforts, repeated often during his favourite
pastime of highlighting remarkable lines in the Bible, with
multi-coloured pens. In this case God's mysteriousness had
provided him with the time to reconsider his attitude to
money, to this money. He had been shown, for the first
time in his life, real poverty.

The spending plan, to begin with, had been simple. Half
the money was earmarked for worthy charities (such as the

sending of Bibles in Serbo-Croat to Bosnian refugees, and in
Somali to the famine victims), and the other half was to be
used to establish himself as a missionary in the jungles of
Brazil. In preparation for this, his first act on hearing of his
father's death had been to buy himself a set of tapes which
should have taught him Portuguese in seven weeks. There
was no reference to redemption in the language course, or
to salvation or damnation, and that had troubled him for an
hour or two, until he came to his senses and chided himself
for his lack of faith. The words were not important. His faith
would shine through and do the work for him.

He was not terribly worried by losing his job in the middle
of June. The money, his solicitor told him, was imminent.
The period of redundancy would give him extra time for
study and prayer before he flew to Rio. If anything, it
was a relief that he would no longer have to defend his
profession to the more extreme young Turks at his church.
Some of them had considered word-processing for a tabloid
newspaper to be a morally outrageous occupation. These
whited sepulchres tended to be individuals who served God
on social security, but Virgil had never pointed that out to
them, knowing, he told himself, something of the practice
of true charity.

The bank tired of his overdraft and promises some time
in September and his landlord began to threaten eviction
in October. Throughout November baked beans and pasta
became his locusts and honey, and the lack of heating in
the flat made it a desert for him. Every morning he thanked
God for this humbling experience, before crossing the road
to the phone box to see if the money was through yet.
He had no doubt that God had sent these trials so that he
would have some understanding of the exigencies faced by
his future flock. The days took on a meditative rhythm, as he
coloured in the few remaining blank passages in his Bible, to
kill the time between Richard and Judy and the Australian
soaps. The evenings were not a problem. There was usually

an evangelical meeting somewhere in South London, and the long walks there and back were good for the soul.

The day before the money came through, the offices of the organisation which sent Bibles to Bosnia and Somalia were raided by the Fraud Squad. A close personal friend of Virgil's was arrested. Virgil took the timing of this as a sign from God, said a prayer for the blackened soul of his friend, and hoped that he himself wasn't mentioned in the organisation's records. He was shocked by the degree of naivety he had demonstrated in committing himself to that cause, and decided to do something about it. A man who saw goodness in everything would not last long in Brazil. As far as he could tell, from the shelves of his local bookshop, there were no self-help guides on how not to be a sucker. He decided that he would have to achieve worldly wisdom by a more direct approach. He would spend his first evening of wealth in the West End, observing sinners in action.

Soho seemed a likely place to start. A friend of his who used to testify outside Tottenham Court Road station had once told him that Soho was the world's epicentre of depravity. The friend was reluctant to specify what form this depravity took but, since all sin was damnation, any kind of sin would do. Virgil pinned his money into his pocket with a safety-pin and took the Northern Line to Leicester Square. He said the Lord's Prayer three times between the tube and Cambridge Circus, and then began to reflect on other matters.

It was still afternoon, but even so he felt out of place walking down Old Compton Street in his waxed jacket and corduroys. He decided that his first investment should be in some clothes which would help him to blend in with the crowd a little more. He found a respectable-looking shop, the window of which was not festooned with leather brassières on male mannequins and, heady at the prospect of spending money for the first time since June, entered.

The assistant, by practising the shop assistant's art, made

him feel six inches tall within three minutes. He couldn't find a price tag on any of the clothes and was too embarrassed to ask, knowing too that with the amount of money he had in his pocket a few pounds either way wouldn't make any difference. He chose some black things with DOLCE & GABBANA written across the front of them in large white letters, such as he had seen other young men wearing in the street. Black suited him, he told himself. It was rather priestly, in fact, and wouldn't go to waste in his life as a preacher. Once he was wearing his new outfit; with his old clothes bagged on the counter, the assistant rang them up and asked for an amount of money which was as much as he had in his pocket. There was no turning back without an unbearable loss of face, so he paid and left the shop, muttering a prayer to himself to stem the inexplicable elation he felt as he searched for a cash machine.

Finding a den of sin was not as easy as he had expected. There were places with painted women sitting in the front, but they did not appeal to him or seem appropriate. He couldn't be certain that entering such a place would not involve some kind of participation, and he was here as an observer, purely. He went into bars, but they were full of clean, good-looking young men who seemed to have nothing but goodwill to express to each other. Indeed, some of them were openly embracing in much the way that he and his friends embraced at church meetings. And some of them wore large silver crosses around their necks. Unused to drink, by eight o'clock Virgil was under the impression that he was among his own kind.

At a place called Crews, which had been recommended to him by a man in a kilt who was not, it transpired, Scottish, he fell into conversation with a lad of about his own age, who said that he was a model and who, within ten minutes, had told Virgil that he liked him very much. Virgil then felt confident enough to mention the legacy, which was an opening for the young man to hint at how broke he was.

Virgil said that was fine: he had enough money for both of them, if the other would consent to show him around.

Warren, which was the name of Virgil's new friend, put the seal on Virgil's confidence when he replied to this request by saying that they were all going to heaven. It wasn't until much later, when they were in the place, that Virgil realised that Heaven was a nightclub, but by then he was too drunk and full of goodwill to care.

He was smiling and looking round him at the thick crowd of whooping, grinning men, dancing bare-chested with one another. There was no sign of any sin that he recognised. There was, admittedly, the occasional girl in suspiciously erotic clothing but, since the men seemed to be taking no notice, the atmosphere was not spoiled by their presence. Warren seemed to know half the people there, and introduced him freely. Virgil said something about being part of a new community, but he was slurring, and the music was loud, and his remark went unnoticed.

With some urgency, Warren asked him for thirty quid, and disappeared into one of the arches by the dance floor once it was in his hand. When he returned he handed Virgil what looked like an aspirin, and took one himself.

'I was beginning to have a bit of a headache,' Virgil said. 'Thanks.'

He wondered about asking what the thirty quid had been for, but Warren had started to dance and it seemed a mean and churlish question. He tried to dance for a while without much success, and then he felt the music come at him, not through his ears, but across the floor and up his legs. The next thing he knew he was holding on to Warren and feeling an incredible affection for all the world. Warren asked him if the White Dove had come up yet, and that was when he knew that he was full of the spirit.

'I love London,' he said. 'I never knew that all this was going on, under my nose. This is like, like real religion.

In action, you know? God moves, God moves. God moves something, you know what I mean.'

Warren agreed that it was a good one and told him to take deep breaths.

A week later, when he caught the plane to Rio, Warren came with him. He still had vague missionary intentions, but Warren assured him that the Copacabana was where all the real sinners were, and that it was more comfortable than the jungle, so they stayed there. There was, Virgil told himself, Warren's soul to be saved first of all, and money to burn.

∫

AFTER THE CONQUERING HERO

∫

It was high summer, after the last of the thirty-two dachshunds had gone, when Olivia decided that it was time to leave the house herself. The morning Cosmos had died she was in her deck chair on the terrace, at about the time when Bill would have brought her a glass of sherry before lunch, listening to the inane chatter of the paying visitors, and the decision came to her, or, rather, she admitted the inevitability of it. The plain Georgian façade of the house ascended and spread behind her, dressed in the green of wisteria, the sparse second flush invisible among the leaves but perceptible to the nose through the cloying scents of a hot weather garden.

Fifty-three years had been filled between their coming to this house and the day she found Bill lying on the kitchen floor among his dachshunds. It was wartime when they came, a time of impatience. The house had been shrouded in Victorian additions and wings, and the garden was a desert of pragmatism. But Bill was away in North Africa most of the time and there wasn't the labour for demolition and reconstruction. For four years she had counted butter coupons and made lists and drawn plans and nursed cuttings in ground which patriotism should have given over to cabbages. She had celebrated VE night by taking a sledgehammer into the East Wing and smashing all the windows.

Over the noise of breaking glass she sang the hymn about the coming of the conquering hero, careless of whether anyone should hear, knowing that madness would be forgiven on that mad night. She had dreamt of Bill's return to her for so long that her love had made a conquering hero of him, and she had forgotten the small details of his humanity: that he was a man who feared God and the Conservative Government; that he would commit suicide rather than wear a pair of trousers that were not rolled at the ends. When he had returned she was so glad to see him, and there were so many things to do, that she forgot to question whether she was happy or not. It was an age when such questions were not to be asked and, in any case, she was blessed with the symptoms of happiness.

Within a year of Bill's demobilisation the house had been stripped of its wings and restored to eighteenth-century dignity. There were men wheeling barrows of earth about the garden, and lines of embryonic hedging standing where only imagination could make them appropriate. It all had to be done without wealth, so, by 1950, the public were paying to roam the garden and make inappropriate exclamations over plants they didn't recognise. Often they would ask her the name of a plant.

'Have you got a pencil and notebook,' she would say.

'No.'

'Well in that case I won't bother telling you. You'll only forget as soon as I turn my back.' And she would pick up her trug and stalk away, puffing on her Woodbine, her eyes scanning left and right for the next job which needed her attention.

She had always assumed that Bill would outlive her, since it was she who first succumbed to the symptoms of ageing. Her lungs began to weaken because of her precious Woodbines and arthritis took hold of her hands. In the last few years she felt that she had lost control of the garden, able to reach only two-thirds of it in her electric chariot, and then only when the weather was dry, with Bill striding alongside her and the fluency of dogs galloping around her. Her waning, though she didn't think so at the time, was tolerable while Bill was there.

Under her instruction he became a good cook. Indeed, he died with his striped apron tied around his middle, flaking haddock for a kedgeree, chattering, as always, to the dogs, knowing each of the identical multitude by sight and name. It was the cessation of this chatter which indicated to her that something might be wrong, but by the time she had struggled into the kitchen, calling his name between the labours of each step she took, he was dead, the dogs over and around him in a tadpole mass of snoozing sympathy, single tan eyebrows lifted, here and there, at her presence.

It was plain that she couldn't manage the dogs after he was gone. In ones and twos they went, to carefully chosen homes and breeders. She decided to keep Cosmos, an elderly bitch, for company. Cosmos outlived Bill by six months, until Olivia found her dead in her basket on that summer morning, and realised that there were some frustrations you could not fight against: that love alone could not sustain a life; would not sustain the life of the garden, which was dying a slow death, perceptible only to her and to those who knew the garden well; who knew it of old. The garden needed someone young, someone with the energy to carry out a vision, to discard passengers with a disregard for sentiment, and undertake new planting with an eye to the future. It could not be her, nor did she have the strength to watch it happen.

In kindness they had offered her a housekeeper, and in scorn she had answered, 'A woman? Do you think that I could tolerate a woman around the place? I like men and the company of men. I won't be locked in a woman's company and forgotten.'

And George, her nephew, who, perhaps, was the only

one who could understand a sentiment like that, had said that if she ever decided to leave the place she could come and live with him and Michael across the hill. She would be no trouble to them. Indeed, she could advise them on the garden they were making. George and Michael had got to the age when farming, although it kept them busy, was not enough for them, and they were turning the acres nearest the house into a pleasure ground; leaving the sheep and the wheat to the farm manager, while they coaxed fritillaries down grassy slopes and worked out strategies for invisible staking.

The morning of the decision she hauled herself from her deck chair to her electric chariot for a tour of the garden. Not a last tour: she would not be moving this week or the next. She would stay while the weather was good. The structure of the garden still pleased her. She would stop before one vista or another and say to herself, 'Well, I got that right, at least.' But soon she would see a weed where no weed had been in her time, or a chlorotic plant where the soil had been allowed to get out of condition, and her swollen knuckles would tremble with rage and helplessness. Her head gardener had got what she called *The Disease*, and she could see him in the distance, gossiping amiably with a member of the public, oblivious to the undone work at his feet. Of course, if he saw her, there would be a great pantomime of activity, but you only had to look at the garden to see that nothing was done until it was absolutely necessary or, more likely, too late. She turned her chariot towards the house and, once there, telephoned George.

She moved in October, just as the last herbaceous blaze, propped by colchicums, was fading. All that she needed, and she had been surprised by how little that was, had been transferred across the hill. She moved with a semblance of high spirits, only allowing herself to weep in the privacy of her new bedroom. To pretend anything but happiness would have been ungracious; an unkindness to George and

Michael, who had been happy by themselves before her arrival; who, in kindness, had changed a working domestic arrangement for her sake.

To her surprise, happiness came to her, and was not long in the coming. She had been dreaming every night of Bill, and the dogs, and the garden: that was only natural. But it was Michael who brought her out of herself in the daytime. He was a great flirt. He spoke to her and treated her as though she were still a woman, and not the sexless string of bones and wrinkles she appeared to be. At breakfast, on the third day, she was alone with Michael. They watched the retreating aspect of a pleasingly substantial postman as he manoeuvred between the ivy flowers that flanked the path to the gate. Michael turned from the window and said something unremarkable about postmen and honesty.

'Well,' Olivia said, narrowing her eyes at the last glimpse of thigh-stretched navy trousers. 'I'd certainly take him on trussed.'

Michael laughed uproariously.

'I would have thought,' she said, in mild surprise, 'that one would have been a bit old-fashioned for you.'

'What one?' Michael said. He was genuinely puzzled and thought for a minute until he had worked out the *double entendre*. 'Good God. I've just got it. I wasn't laughing at that at all. I was just laughing at the way you said it. Sorry, it's just that I have a dirty laugh.'

'Well,' she said, 'I've got a dirty mind. So that's all right.'

For a moment, she was gripped by a sense of freedom. Much as she had loved Bill, he had been a bit of a prude, and she had spent the whole of her adult life checking herself whenever she felt a risqué utterance forming in her mind. Over the days that followed she tested George and Michael by degrees, until she decided that there was nothing she could say that would shock them. There were times when she worried that this new turn her conversation was taking might be a sign of senility. She had heard of old ladies who had lost their marbles and taken to obscenity. She worried that George and Michael were indulging her rather than enjoying her company. But the proof was that their laughter was always spontaneous and, as far as she could tell, they were laughing with her and not at her.

She discovered new pleasures. She took to watching rugby matches, not out of any interest in the sport, but as an opportunity to make salacious remarks about the players' legs. And when the match was over, she might turn from the television and say, 'I'm sure if they had a camera in the dressing room the viewing figures for this kind of thing would rocket.'

George and Michael would collapse in giggles to hear such a remark made in such a serious, elderly, upper-class voice.

She put on weight under their care, so that her tweed skirts no longer fitted her, and so they introduced her to casual clothing. She bought in cases of good whiskey and they all got a bit squiffy, as she liked to put it, every evening in the small sitting-room, in stretchy cotton trousers and uncontrolled good humour.

'If I'd known it was this much fun here I'd have left Bill and those bloody dogs ages ago.' She spoke as though she didn't mean it, really, but there was a sense in which she did. Michael told her, his eyes vacant as if in a parody of love, that they had never laughed so much until her arrival.

That admission of his was followed by the most fleeting sense of discomfort on her part. She was no longer accustomed to having her usefulness pointed out to her.

Of course, when she died seven weeks after moving over the hill, all her old friends said that she must have died of a broken heart; that having lost Bill and the dogs and the garden in so short a time had left her with nothing to live for; that it must have been hard for her to know that her house was already being converted into a conference centre and the garden re-landscaped on more corporate lines. That she died of a broken heart was technically true, but it had more to do with emphysema than emotion. She had just spent an outrageous evening with George and Michael, having supper in a pub which specialised in male strippers. On reaching home she complained of a headache and had her first stroke while Michael was fetching the aspirin. By the time the ambulance came she was conscious again, and making the most of the happy gas that they were pumping into her. As the ambulance sped over the hills the attendant turned his back on her, and on Michael, who was accompanying her, and she raised the mask from her face for a moment. Michael thought she might have something vital to impart. She had already acknowledged, while waiting for the ambulance, that she was about to die.

But there was a gleam in her eye, and she winked at Michael while jerking her thumb in the direction of the attendant. She mouthed the word, 'cute'.

A moment later the attendant, who was, admittedly, extraordinarily handsome, was at her side again, being professionally solicitous and asking her if she was comfortable. She raised her mask slightly and said in a pathetic voice that her right leg ached and could he rub it for her.

While the medic obliged she made scandalous eyes at Michael, who had to bury his face in his hands to disguise his giggling fit as a surge of grief.

On arrival at the hospital she refused to sign the consent form for an operation. Twenty minutes later she was dead. Her ashes, naturally, were placed next to Bill's, beneath his suitably dignified headstone.

∫

HANDSOME MEN ARE SLIGHTLY
SUNBURNT

∫

Katie lived at the top of the lowering grey town that rose, on a steep hill, from the river. Her house stank sweet with decay. The only parts of it that were clear or clean were tracks along the floor between the rooms, where Katie had dragged herself on her bottom for the past thirty years. On fine days she would sit out on the doorstep for the company of passing traffic and children. There was a fat brown and white spaniel called Barney who visited her at the same time each afternoon, and sat with her while she fed him fig rolls or coconut creams. She got the Meals-on-Wheels but, aside from that, as far as anyone could tell, she lived on biscuits and tea. What she did about the other end of things was a great mystery. There had never been a lavatory in the house, and no one had the indelicacy to ask a question like that of a small woman of such dignity and independence.

She went in one of those hot months that do not happen every year in County Wexford. A month when she had been long hours on her threshold beaming her smile and blinking in the sunshine; when the passing people seemed to have more time to stop with her, as if time had been slowed by the strength of the heat. A time of long mornings when people walked with the limpidness of foreigners, temporarily forgetting that their anatomies had evolved for scuttling through rainstorms, and of evenings which stayed light until near closing time, when the pubs were full of pinkened sandy drinkers, on weekends when the population of the town had flooded down to the seaside and back again. She liked the smell of hot tar off the road and was not yet so short-sighted that she couldn't see who went into Langan's bar across the way, and how they came out of it.

Young men, like Emmet Marshall, would nod to her in passing and ask her how she was, their skins glowing in the evening, on their return from Carnivan, the strand where all the real townspeople went to take their sunshine. And she would answer that she was grand, boy, grand, and hadn't it been a lovely day now, thank God. And Emmet, or it might be his cousin, Brian, would pass along to their grandmother's big house two doors down, and push against a door that they had never known to be locked in waking hours. And say hello to the aunt and go to the tin and take a lump of whatever cake was in it and make their way to the foot of the square wooden bed. Elbows rested on the bedstead and mouth full of cake, ready to tell the soft gossip of the summer, and hear what they had missed in the town that day: who had died and who had nearly died and who had been taken up to John of God's for the cure.

Emmet Marshall's grandmother would rouse herself from her doze over the crossword upon his entrance and, giving his face a matter-of-fact glance of appraisal, would begin the conversation by saying, 'handsome men are slightly sunburnt'. No matter that by now he was deeply tanned, the compliment was still given, and he would take it with the becoming sheepishness of youth. It was a phrase that came from somewhere in her childhood, and she had used it all the summers he could remember, from when he was small enough to believe anything she said. She used, in his days of credulity, to show him her few remaining strands of red hair and thrill him by telling him that she had been a tinker girl before she married his grandfather. There were elaborate stories of travels with an ass and cart, and of saucepan mending, and beautiful lies of her being wooed by the well-dressed man from the town on account of her long flaming hair. The child Emmet would listen, in a cataract of detail which allowed no room for questions.

The fictions for the child had now become, with no decrease in volubility, facts for the man. At eighteen and back from Carivan he listened as she told him what visitors she had had that day, and what the visitors had had to say for themselves. Every few minutes her hearing aid would whistle and she would put a hand behind her ear to adjust it, swearing like a navvy. It astonished him sometimes that she had news to tell; that anyone got a word in at all from the foot of her bed. It could only be that she was a creature of extrapolation and that she could read novels in the monosyllables which she occasionally allowed to others.

He would stay in her company until it was time to change into a white shirt and make his way down to the Royal Hotel, where he would serve behind the main bar until eleven and, on disco nights, behind the bar upstairs until three. The pay wasn't great, but it was good summer work, since it left you free to be outdoors in the daytime.

The evening of the big fire in Brogue Lane he arrived in her room expecting her to have all the details, but she seemed preoccupied with other matters.

'Did you hear about the fire?' he said.

'Mrs Hammond was up telling me about it. Wasn't it terrible? She brought me the flowers out of her garden. Aren't they lovely?'

She indicated a bowl of roses on her bedside table. He had taken no notice of them until that moment. She always had flowers there and, to him, one bloom was much like another, camouflaged among the clutter that she needed to have within her reach.

'There's one of them is a bit like a rose I had years ago. I lost it since, but I remember sending a slip of it down to Katie in the war. I'd lay any money it's in her garden still. We'll find out soon enough, I suppose.'

There was an uncharacteristically long pause in her talk while she studied the rose, a small pale pink thing of the kind that could hardly be desired but might be treasured once it was owned. Emmet wondered what was about to happen that would give them access to Katie's garden. But he didn't ask, since he had deduced from his grandmother's tone that he should know already.

'I've been thinking what we're to do with Katie's house,' she said.

For a moment, in his alarm, he couldn't remember whether he had seen Katie on her doorstep that evening. Perhaps he hadn't noticed her absence, being preoccupied by the curls of smoke from the direction of Brogue Lane.

'She isn't dead, is she?' he said. It was a natural question, in a town where the last rites seemed to outnumber all the other sacraments put together.

His grandmother scorched him with a look. 'You're a great listener,' she said, sarcastically. 'It's been common knowledge the last month they're moving her up to the new estate. The poor craythur won't know where she is.'

'Right,' Emmet said, unheeded by his grandmother, who went on to speculate how Katie might cope with running water and electricity and all the essentials she had always lived without in apparent contentment.

At the next lull in her flow he said, 'So what has her house to do with us?'

'It's mine,' she said, with astonishment at how little her grandson knew of the business of others. 'It's the last of the houses your grandfather bought, God rest him.' And then she was away, having caught hold of the subject of her dead husband's goodness, and how he used to sing to her in bed every morning (the aunts had pronounced this a fantasy), and how there hadn't been a pauper in town whom he wouldn't go out of his way to help (and that was allowed by the aunts to be true).

Emmet had faint memories of his grandfather, a harassed man who had given him half a crown on Sundays to buy ice-cream. There was a vague recollection of the discovery, after his death, that he had owned several small houses in the town. Apparently he had the habit, whenever he heard of an impending eviction, of buying the house in question and allowing the tenant to continue to live in it rent free. Though he had not been a wealthy man he had been comfortable by the standards of the town and, in any case, none of the houses had been of the kind that commanded a great price in those days. And, being modest in his goodness, not even his family had known of these purchases until the reading of his will.

Rather than ask more questions of his grandmother and give her the great satisfaction she would derive from his ignorance, Emmet just listened, piecing the story together from the unnecessary detail in her speech and half-remembered dribs of family gossip.

She had a proposition for him. The house was not worth selling or renting in its present condition, and she had made enough money from the sale of the back field to do it up nicely. What had been considered a slum dwelling fifty years ago was now ideal accommodation for the kind of girl who came to work in the banks. Two or three quiet, single girls could share it and pay a good rent between them. First, the house had to be cleared and that was something Emmet could do. She would pay him well. She knew that he was saving money to go travelling on the Continent before the summer was out.

'You needn't be paying me, Gran. It's no bother. I'll do it anyway.'

'I wouldn't be asking you if I wasn't going to pay you,' she said. 'It'll be hard work.'

*   *   *

Two days later Katie was gone and, by all accounts, delighted with her new lifestyle. She boiled the electric kettle twenty times a day for the pleasure of it. There were still schoolchildren to pass her doorway in the afternoon, though not so much traffic, and she still sat beaming on the threshold. Barney somehow rediscovered her, and everyone said the dog was a marvel, and the half mile trot up the hill to the new estate for his fig roll helped to mitigate the effect of the biscuit on his waistline.

Once his grandmother had spent an enjoyable morning on the telephone negotiating the hire of the skip, Emmet set to work. The task was destructive enough to be satisfying and sufficiently archaeological to be interesting. There were rotten stair banisters to be kicked down and layers of paint and wallpaper so thick that the rooms they were taken from seemed twice the volume once they were stripped. Stacks of papers and magazines and calendars that went back to the beginning of the century were sorted through but, in the end, thrown away in their entirety. Katie's hoarding had been so indiscriminate that any separation of the worthwhile was no task for a man working in full spate, and within two hours Emmet had become more bulldozer than human. He worked in a frenzy, his blood up, sweating in the baking heat and choking in clouds of dust and plaster dust. When he could no longer breathe he would retreat to the yard and saw down ash trees that were sprouting from the foundations, and hack down brambles and Russian vine; all the time keeping an eye out for the rose bush his grandmother claimed had once grown there and was there still. He had no doubt of the rose's existence, because he believed that his grandmother had the power to know things she had never witnessed. She might fantasise about the past, but her knowledge of the present was keen and hard and independent of anything so banal as fact.

The only incident which blighted the euphoria of the work happened halfway through the first morning. He was standing by an open window upstairs contemplating, for a moment, the wall that was to be the next victim of berserk improvement. Two women had stopped in the street and were peering into the house.

'Shocking,' said one.

'And the money them Marshalls have.'

'That's the way. Them that have it hang on to it.'

'Still, you'd think they'd have been ashamed of themselves to be keeping the poor old thing in them conditions.'

He reported the conversation to his grandmother at lunchtime, expecting her rage to match his own. But she shrugged her shoulders. 'I'd expect no less. We gave the woman a roof over her head when her own family wouldn't come up the street to make her a cup of tea. The only way to get thanks in this town is to do nothing.'

And then she eased herself astride a hobby horse and began reciting her lines as though she had learned them as a schoolchild: how there had been women in the town who would get up at seven and sweep the path outside their front doors to gain the reputation of being great housekeepers, before going back to bed for the morning while the dirt piled up in their kitchens; how the women who really did keep clean houses never had time to be sweeping the pavements and were considered slovenly as a result (but not how she had had the leisure to observe all this because there was always someone to do her housework for her). Then, with the smoothness of a practised link, her talk turned to wives who belittled their husbands in public. He could have, almost, mimed her words as she spoke them, particularly the profound piece of advice that always came at the end.

'If you ever find yourself married to a woman who does that: just let her belittle you the once, just the once, and you're to hit her a clout, as hard as you can, and walk out the door and never go back to her. Because, once a woman has that in her, there's no cure for it, and you'll never be happy with her. Promise me that much, boy.'

'Yes, Gran.' There was no point in saying more. You couldn't argue with her at the best of times, and her least palatable opinions were her most sacred. He waited for her instructions on choosing a wife, which often followed hard on the incitement to marital violence, but this time they didn't come. The crux of her advice, when it was given, was that to marry outside his class would be to invite disaster. This might have had some basis in logic, except that his grandmother's ideas of class were so constrained that any alliance permitted by her would be forbidden by the law as incestuous.

Instead, she said, 'You're looking tired. Is the work going well?'

'Grand.' He straightened his back so as not to look tired.

Towards the end of the morning, on the second day, with the skip already three-quarters full, Brian put his head round the door to see how the work was progressing. Emmet's cousin was a year and a bit younger than him, but close enough in sensibility for the two to be able to talk, and far enough behind him in experience for them to have something to talk about. Emmet stopped working and put the sledgehammer down, sitting himself on a pile of rubble.

'Rather you than me,' Brian said, taking in the wreckage.

'It's clear enough now. You should have seen it yesterday. The woman never threw anything out. Have you seen the skip in the yard?'

They went outside, and expletives were muttered over the skip and its contents.

'You saved nothing?' Brian said.

'What was good was half rotten and what wasn't would take a lifetime to separate. I thought it may as well all go while I was at it.'

'Still, it's terrible to see a woman's life on a skip.'

'Anything she wanted she must have taken with her.'

'I suppose.'

Despite what he had said, Emmet felt there was a sadness in looking at what was in the skip, and in thinking of the vigorous carelessness with which he had thrown the stuff away. There was nothing of value, but a lot that had been precious. For some reason he thought of the rose, hoping he would find it, as if that might mitigate his brutal handling of Katie's past.

Brian said, 'You look thirsty. Will you knock off for a pint across the road?'

Emmet went into the house and looked for his shirt, wiping his face with it before putting it on. 'That'll do,' he said. 'The more rakish the more takish.'

So it was that he entered Langan's bar with the glow of labour and sunburn about him. After he had brought the pints back to the table he nodded towards the bar and asked Brian who the girl standing behind it was.

'Surely you know Fiona. She used to have longer hair. Old Langan's niece. She has a job here for the summer.'

'She seems fairly friendly.' Emmet smiled over at the smiling barmaid, wondering why, if Brian knew so much about her, he had never noticed her before. She had the looks of a Langan: the square chin and the good teeth. His appraisal might have stopped there if she hadn't come out from behind the bar, ostensibly to collect empty glasses from the tables.

'Working hard?' she said, eyeing the dust on Emmet's boots. 'It's a bit hot for that kind of carry on.'

Emmet heard himself say, 'It's the heat that gets your juices up.' He was surprised by the salaciousness in his own voice. She laughed at him flirtatiously and gave the table she had cleared a perfunctory wipe.

When she was safely behind the bar again Brian spoke

out of the corner of his mouth. 'You're a fast worker.' He was looking at Emmet with sly admiration.

Emmet felt there was nothing to do but take the compliment. He was not, in his own experience, a fast worker, or anything like it, when it came to that sort of thing. A few words of banter with a seemingly lascivious girl on a hot day were not going to change that. But working hard and feeling healthy and making money had given him a self-confidence to which he was not accustomed. He thought he might be letting Brian down if he made a denial of sexual charisma. He said nothing.

Brian took his silence for self-assurance, and said, 'I bet you a tenner you couldn't get her into bed within the week.'

Emmet laughed, at the ludicrousness of the bet, and at Brian's misreading of the situation. He knew that Brian would interpret the laughter differently; that in his excitable virginity he would hear only the hunting cry of the sexually successful male. This did not seem the time to disillusion him with the reality; with half-formed concepts of romantic love.

'You're on,' he said, mentally putting aside the tenner as something already lost.

You might say that it was a whirlwind romance. He asked her if she was going down to the disco at the Royal that night, and she said that she might be, and both of them contrived to make it seem as casual as possible. He said that he worked behind the bar there, and she said that she knew that already.

By ten that evening he was regretting Brian's wager. If she didn't appear he would lose face, and if she did come her appearance would be marred by the bet. He liked her enough to want anything that might happen between them to be on his own terms and in his own time. When he saw her come in the door at the disco the pleasure he felt was tainted with shame. He wanted to sleep with her, but not for the sake of a ten pound note. She sat at the bar counter, fending off the local Romeos and chatting to Emmet whenever he had a moment to stand still, and he, under the pressure of it, found himself putting sly vodkas into the glass of Coke he kept for himself under the counter.

It was about half past three when they walked up the hill together, and the linking of their arms was unpremeditated. So too was the way in which their arms remained linked at the point where she should have turned for her own house but came with him instead to his grandmother's.

'It's coffee I suppose,' he said.

'I suppose,' she said.

He felt awkward putting the kettle on, and worse when he said to her, 'I have to go upstairs for a minute. She gets worried if she's awake and I don't look in.'

He put his head round his grandmother's door. She was asleep in the lamplight, propped up on her pillows, her glasses halfway down her nose and a heavy book open on her chest. Although he had made no noise, he had been standing there only a couple of seconds when her soft snoring gave way to a start and her eyes opened.

'Howiyah,' he said. 'I just got in.'

'Are you on your own?'

He might have been astonished by the question, but he knew, from years of experience, that little could be hidden from her, despite her deafness and confinement. You had to be careful when you chose the shade of whiteness of your lies.

'No,' he said. 'One of the lads came in with me. We're having coffee. Do you want anything?'

If she had asked, as she normally would, who his visitor was he would have been put on the spot, but she let it pass and switched off her hearing aid as a token gesture of cynicism.

'No,' she said, settling down in the bed and putting her glasses and book to one side. 'Thanks for asking. Don't be up talking all night. The skip man is coming in the morning.'

Fiona Langan had skin that was faintly freckled without being pale, and a sort of asymmetry that came from one of her nipples being inverted, though it could pop out if she became excited enough. Emmet decided that it was this nipple which made him as lustful as he was, writhing illicitly on the sitting-room carpet, fourteen feet below the head of his sleeping grandmother. When, after half an hour of them doing every other thing they could think of and of him feeling that if they didn't fuck soon he would burst, she told him that she had never had an orgasm with a man, he did burst, clenching his teeth so that what might have been a roar was no more than a grunt.

'Sorry,' he said. 'I got a bit carried away.'

She observed the pool of sperm by her hip bone and said, 'It's just as well. I'm not on the pill.'

He suggested fetching his condoms out of their hiding place, and knew instantly from her expression that he had said the wrong thing.

'I'm not doing it with those yokes,' she said. 'Don't be disgusting.'

He took her head in his hands hoping, somehow, to bring her back to a state of mind where the concept of disgust would not figure. 'I felt I let you down, that's all,' he said. 'I wanted to make it up to you. There's no reason you shouldn't get as much out of it as I did.'

He kissed her, and for a moment she was tender again, though sad with it. Just as his hand was moving down the flat of her stomach she said, 'I'd better go home. I'll be killed for getting in this late.' And then, having freed herself of his arms, her expression brightened, and she said, 'So what are you doing tomorrow?'

'Work.'

'Me too. Will you be coming at lunchtime?'

'Into Langan's? I could. I have the night off, though. What are you doing?'

'I suppose I could skive off in a good cause.'

'I'll think of something.'

By that time they were both smiling, retrieving garments from across the floor and restoring themselves to a state of dress which would make conversation easier between people who, however intimate they had been, barely knew each other.

When she had gone and he, upstairs, had undressed again, he spent some time in front of the glass before getting into bed, trying to decide whether he was handsome or not. Older women thought he was, and said so, but there was no great satisfaction in being attractive to people who were wise enough to look beyond the superficial. He wasn't interested in whether he was thought to be a good person: he was as good as he felt he needed to be, and he knew it without reassurance. His mother used to tell him that he was handsome, but he was a child then and she was somewhat prejudiced. There was no one he knew well enough to ask straight out. In any case, anyone who cared about him would tell him that he was handsome, to spare his feelings, and anyone who didn't care would tell him that he wasn't, to put him in his place.

The image in the mirror changed back and forth between ugly and handsome until, finally, he could discern no more than that he was tired and sunburnt and, remembering that the skip man would arrive in a few hours, that he should get into bed. His last thought before sleep, as he reviewed the events of the evening, was that, whatever else he was, he was not irresistible.

The good weather and the hard work of the morning brought him to his senses and for a few days he and Fiona went about like any other couple who were going out together. They slow-danced at the Five Counties disco and walked in the early evenings, talking easily and not questioning their liking for each other. The opportunity didn't seem to arise for another frenzied tussle on the sitting room carpet, though they spoke, from time to time, of curing her ignorance of coital orgasm, as thought it were assumed between them that it was something which would happen naturally, in due course.

Brian handed him a tenner one day, assuming, without asking, that that had been the way things had gone. Emmet took the money without comment, making it understood by the gravity of his demeanour that what had once been a joke was now serious and private. The bet, though regrettable, had to be honoured, one way or another. Emmet reasoned that silence on the matter would bring the least dishonour possible to the subject of the bet.

Brian spoiled things by asking him whether he would go on seeing her now the money was won. All Emmet could answer was, 'I'll see how things go, I suppose.'

Sunday was the last good day before the weather broke. Like a couple they rode bicycles out to The Rower for the afternoon, such ease between them that he sang as they cycled and she made no remark on his tunelessness, seeming not to notice it in her happiness. As they returned a light drizzle fell on them, and she said that rainwater was a good hair conditioner, and it somehow never occurred to them that the best of the summer might be over. As they dismounted at the gates of her house he proposed that she should accompany him to Dublin the following weekend.

If he had had an ear for the minute details of town gossip he might have known what to expect when she brought him into her house that day. It was known that her mother had gone several times for the cure, with no sign of improvement. Mrs Langan's condition was of the quiet, homely kind that stopped at her threshold. She had won a certain amount of respect and sympathy for her containment of it, in a town where it seemed that no family was untouched by the problem and no citizen could be unaware of the depths to which it could bring you.

Mrs Langan seemed inordinately pleased to see Emmet, and said at once, 'You're the image of your father,' as though that was the greatest compliment that could be bestowed.

'I know,' was all Emmet could reply. His acknowledgment sounded ungracious in the light of her enthusiasm, but there was no way of telling her that he was being as polite as he could bear to be.

She offered him a drink, making an unsteady gesture towards the sideboard with her own glass, and told him to help himself. Fiona said something about having to get changed, which was the reason they had stopped by, and left them together in the room. As she went he looked for a trace of embarrassment on her features. He could see none. He knew from his own experience that embarrassment would be long gone, replaced by irritation, and that irritation was easier to mask.

The sideboard was well equipped, as though life in this house were one long cocktail party. There was even a bucket of ice and a sliced lemon fanned out in a saucer.

While he had his back turned Mrs Langan said, 'How is your father these days?'

'Grand. I think. I don't see much of him. I'm stopping at Granny's.'

He found her eyes riveted to his face when he turned towards her. 'He was a great looker in our day. Always had a good colour on him. Out, chasing sheep with his da. That was long before he met your mother, God rest her. I never knew her very well.'

'She never liked the town much,' he said, knowing that, although he was putting it mildly, it would turn the tables and return some of the discomfort which she had been inflicting on him.

'You'll have to tell him I was asking after him.'

He thought, out of hope, that might be the end of the subject, but when he glanced at her he could see a disturbingly weepy look to her eyes. He had been wondering how she managed to keep the house and herself in such good condition; such cleanliness and order. There was something pathetic about the carefulness of her appearance, as though, every morning, she had to prove to herself that she had some dignity left, and as though there was dignity in smartness alone.

'I was very fond of him,' she said. 'Did he ever tell you I did a line with him?'

'No.' Emmet couldn't imagine his father mentioning anything so personal, so human.

'It was a long time ago.'

He tried not to show his alarm. He had no wish to hear more about his father's youth, or to hear comparisons and have it implied that he and his father were the same at the same age. It was bad enough looking like the man and being identifiable all over town as Jimmy Marshall's son, without the abandoned entanglements of Jimmy Marshall's youth weeping over him as though he were Jimmy Marshall reborn. He prayed that Fiona would return before things got out of hand, and Fiona did. Having swapped one pair of jeans for another and stuck a brush through her hair she was ready to go out for the night. He put his half empty glass down on the sideboard and began to back towards the door.

'Thanks for the drink. It was lovely meeting you.'

'You're not going off on me already?'

'Sorry. We're late. I said to Gran I'd be back by half past.' He didn't say half past what, since he wasn't wearing a watch and had no idea what time it was.

'You'll have to come back for a proper visit. Fiona, I was telling him about when I used to go out with his dad. Next time I'll get the photos out and you'll stay longer.'

As they walked up Bewley Street with his bicycle between

them they spoke of the coincidence of their parents having been sweethearts once, ignoring the more patent thing which they had in common. He knew how she would be feeling about it: that she would be entertaining the futile hope that he had noticed nothing out of the ordinary; had thought her mother was doing nothing more than having a well earned little drink on a Sunday afternoon. He didn't want to tell her that he knew how she felt, because that would entail his admission that he knew how he himself felt, and that admission was still a long way in the future.

'God,' he said. 'What if they'd got married?'

'Apparently,' she said, 'they nearly did.'

'You knew about it?'

'She started talking about it the minute she heard that I was going out with you.'

'You never told me.'

'It didn't seem important.'

'It isn't. It's just funny, is all. Odd. Not that I'm anything like him or you're anything like her.'

'Maybe,' she said. 'God knows what they were like at our age.'

'People don't change,' he said, more because he wished it than because he had had the time to observe it.

And she agreed with him, because if it was true that people couldn't change then her mother was blameless. Pitying the helpless is less of a strain than railing against the obstinate.

He finished clearing Katie's house that week. A rose bush did emerge from the undergrowth at the back of the house, gnarled and decrepit enough to have been planted during the war. The bush was blind, so there was no way of telling if it was the right rose or not. Under his grandmother's instruction he took cuttings from it and planted them in a pot which she kept on her bedroom windowsill. She discussed the rose so earnestly, with everyone who came to see her, that he wished, for her sake, it was the right

one, or that if it was another rose she would be dead
before it flowered and never know the disappointment
of it. She was not a woman upon whom you would wish
disappointment.

It was a week of steady rain, and there was no new
sunburn by which his grandmother could remark upon
his handsomeness in the evenings, but Fiona looked at him
from time to time as though she took pleasure in what she
was seeing and that, in some ways, was better.

Each time he saw her he felt a little warmer towards her.
There was nothing too girlie or pretentious about her. If
they came to a barbed wire fence while out walking she
would cross it without comment, not flapping or shrieking
the way that most girls would. If he said what was on his
mind she would not seize on it as though she had been
waiting to be offended all along. There was nothing in it
that could be called love, on his part, but having known
love once he was in no great hurry to repeat the agonies
of that state.

They looked forward to the weekend in Dublin. There
was a party to go to on the Saturday, and a flat they
could have to themselves while his older brother was away
pursuing some indelicate liaison of his own. The freedom
of a double bed where they could have sex like adults and
not have to neck like adolescents.

At the end of the week he reminded his grandmother that
he would be away, and she asked him where he would be
staying, and he told her.

'Is Fiona going up with you?'

'Yes.'

'And where will she be staying?'

'I don't know. Some friends of hers I suppose.'

He had spoken the lie that was required of him. Whether
she believed it or not was immaterial. She asked him if
he was all right for money, and he said that he was, and
she gave him some anyway so that, she said, he wouldn't

have to be dipping into his savings. Knowing that he had no choice in the matter he took it without a struggle of conscience.

He sensed the change before they arrived in Dublin. Or so it seemed in retrospect. Not that she changed in any way, but that was the problem. She remained the same while he and the world about them changed. Though he saw it at once he did not acknowledge it for twenty-four hours. He had other things on his mind: an itch for consummation and the sudden freedom of a city.

The rain was heavier in Dublin and as steady, and his brother's flat was darkened with it. Over the double bed there was a semi-erotic photograph which might pass for art if a difficult question were asked. The sheets were clean, which was only noticeable in contrast to the state of everything else. They decided it was too wet to go out for food, but he managed to find enough scrags and ends in the kitchen cupboards to put together a sort of pasta supper that wasn't bad. They ate to the sound of a wet Alsatian guard dog howling from the rooftops and a distant, ignored, burglar alarm. They went to bed, and they went so far, and she said, 'No.'

'What's the matter?'

'I might get pregnant.'

Before he had time to think about the advantages of not sounding cross he had said, 'I thought you would have sorted all that out by now. You've had plenty of time.' By then there was no way of salvaging the situation, but still he took a deep breath and said, 'Look. I brought the condoms. Just in case.'

'I told you. I won't do it with those.'

'Why not?'

'I just won't. They're not reliable. I had a fright once.'

'For Christ's sake,' he said. 'It was you wanted the fucking orgasm.'

When she wept he held her, although he was almost shaking with his own rage, or perhaps his lust; it was hard to tell. She fell asleep and he stayed awake, holding her and hating her and trying to find reasons for it. It seemed that the whole weekend had been spoiled already, and he regretted having asked her along.

All the next day, every time he looked at her, she seemed out of place. He spoke to her as little as possible and, when he did, he spoke sharply. It was when she put on a pair of dungarees to wear to the party that his sudden dislike of her found a focus. She asked him if she looked all right, and he said that she did, without looking at her. He wondered how he had never noticed before how unsophisticated she was; how he could have ended up doing a line with such a culchie. At home the dungarees had looked fine; had seemed like anti-fashion chic, but here, among friends who knew better, they were just inappropriate.

He ignored her at the party while he talked to a girl who told him that he had a great tan, and who was prepared to argue the demerits of Bunyan with him. They were laughing about the puddles and the horsepads when Fiona came up to them. He had noted, with a terrible satisfaction, that she had found no one to talk to, and he knew, maliciously, that the conversation he was engaged in would be beyond her. She asked him for the keys to the flat and said that she'd had enough. He handed the keys over and carried on his conversation as though he barely knew her.

She was gone when he returned in the morning, prepared, in the euphoria of conquest, to be quite civilised about the whole thing. There was a note on the door saying that the keys were with a neighbour. If it ever crossed his mind, in the time that followed, that he should make any amends, he never got the chance. Although you wouldn't think it possible, in a town that small and that lowering, he never saw her again.

∫

OLDCOURT

∫

The animals never aged in that household. They came young – pups, kittens, guinea pigs, the odd tortoise – and some managed to make it to maturity but none ever survived into decrepitude. Bell had been with them four years and her life was something of a record, but there were worries about her now that she was pregnant. Either of the dogs at the neighbouring farm might have been responsible. If it was the terrier, as it had been the last time, she would be fine. If it was the sheepdog there might be trouble. She was so bloated now that the latter case was suspected. There was talk sometimes of taking her to the vet, but it joined all the other talk of things that were never done. The small dog carried her burden with no apparent concern, as if she hadn't noticed that there was something wrong.

Being the day it was, there should, at least, have been nuts and apples in the house. Not that anyone had a particular passion for nuts, but it was traditional. It seemed that in other years there had been mounds of hazelnuts and walnuts and Brazil nuts and the sound of their cracking would go on all evening, their shells being thrown into the fire, on the grate of which a row of chestnuts roasted and blackened. The apples were more for playing with than for eating: an excuse for throwing water around and winning money. Roy disliked the apple games. He couldn't bear to get wet, and the frustration of trying to catch the things in your mouth, which the others found so hilarious, was just frustration to him. And it seemed, when he did bite them, that he always got the pennies or just a mouthful of apple, while the others got shillings and sixpences. Still, at least the nuts and apples separated Halloween from all the other nights of the year, and caused laughter in the house. They almost cried with it the night his mother absentmindedly put the shell in her mouth and threw the nutcrackers on the fire.

This year they had the basins of water ready and the strings hung in the doorway from four o'clock in the afternoon. The younger ones had themselves twisted into knots of impatience.

'When can we start?'

'When your daddy comes home with the nuts.'

'Will he be home soon?'

'Soon.'

Roy followed his mother to the kitchen. Without needing to be asked he took a wire cooling rack from the cupboard and placed it on the table, while his mother took the barm brack from the oven. The air was filled with the rich smell of it. Somewhere inside the cake there would be a wedding ring and a sixpence. It seemed that Roy always got the wedding ring in his slice. The sixpence, foretelling wealth, had gone to just about everyone else over the years.

'I wonder,' his mother said, 'if you'll get the ring again.'

'I don't want to be married. I want to stay with you when I'm grown up.'

'You'll soon get over that.'

He looked at the basins of water on the linoleum and asked, 'What if he isn't home in time?'

Almost under her breath, she said, 'I'll think of something.'

They tried, at about seven, to improvise the games using pears and tomatoes instead of the apples. The substitute fruit didn't work very well, but the tomatoes made enough mess for the exercise to be entertaining. The children ate their barm brack with wet hair and tomato seeds all down their shirts.

'Can we do it again, properly, when Daddy comes home with the apples?'

'We'll see. If he's not too late.'

Roy chewed carefully, and when his teeth hit something hard he prayed for it not to be the wedding ring. He spat sixpence into his hand.

'See,' he said triumphantly. 'I'm not getting married. I'm going to be rich instead.'

He got up and stood behind his mother's chair, whispering in her ear as she poured tea, 'I'll buy a big house. For just the two of us. And a motorbike with a sidecar to drive you round in. Don't tell anyone, so you won't?'

She looked at him for a moment, seeming even more tired now that she was smiling. 'I can't wait,' she said.

They watched television, the younger ones staying up later than usual in case the nuts and apples arrived, his mother dozing through the squabbles. Roy was thinking that it didn't feel like Halloween; that there should be more to it: witches or ghosts or something of that order. It used to be that ghost stories would be told while the nutcracking went on, or his mother would tell them of the Halloweens of her childhood in the town; of dressing up and carrying lamps made of mangels and knocking on neighbours' doors for sweets. Thinking about it, Roy decided that this Halloween was unbearably mundane, and that he should do something about it.

'I'm going upstairs,' he said. 'I've got homework.'

His mother opened her eyes and looked at him warily. No one did homework voluntarily on a Friday evening. But he was out the door before she could say anything, and the evening had got to the point where she would not rise from her chair now until it was time for her to go to bed.

Roy took a clean sheet from the airing cupboard and

opened the bathroom window. Climbing down was more difficult than usual because of the sheet, but he managed by holding it between his teeth. He began to be excited, as though he were engaged in a great adventure and not a small practical joke. He hoped that he would not make a noise as he hit the ground; that Bell would not hear the noise and bark.

Bell was waiting for him at ground level. She whined in an odd way when he petted her. All he could see of her were two small gleams where her eyes would be. He thought she was whining because she was worried about what was going on. Usually when he climbed out of that window at night it was to leave home, and she would accompany him for a couple of miles down the dark lanes, and return with him when he had walked off the anger and decided to give his family another try.

'It's all right,' he whispered. 'I'm not going anywhere. Just be quiet like a good dog.'

Her body felt enormous under his hand, and she was slow to follow him to his chosen station in the middle of the garden.

He already had the sheet over his head when she sat by him. She made the strange little whine again and when he hissed at her to be quiet she went away into the darkness. He was too busy debating with himself whether to stand still or move about to notice her going. He decided that standing still would be best, until he had heard the first screams from the house, and then he could move towards the window in a menacing sort of way. At the last moment, while he was tapping at the window and they were at the height of their terror, he would throw the sheet off and everyone would laugh.

He waited longer than he had expected. Although it was not a particularly cold night he began to feel chilled after forty minutes or so. Still, he stood there, thinking that any minute now someone must look out of a window. It was

Halloween after all, and that was the sort of thing he did himself: look out of windows every so often to check that there was nothing supernatural happening in the garden. He had seen what might have been ghosts that way; strange shapes moving beneath the pear trees. Now that there was a real, large, white ghost in the garden someone, surely, must notice it. He began to be a little afraid, in case the true ghosts should resent an imposter. This Oldcourt landscape should be riddled with ghosts: it had once been a parish and was now no more than two households, and neither of them within screaming distance of the other. He began to be more than a little afraid, but still he held his ground.

It was the sound of a car engine that moved him. He knew that the disguise would not stand up to the glare of headlights, and he suspected that his father might not understand the joke. He pulled the sheet off and ran towards the house, trying to fold it as he ran. The fear of being caught and of looking stupid replaced all other fears and he scaled the wall onto the porch roof in record time. Inside the bathroom he checked the sheet to see if it would give evidence against him. It was clean still, but there was a small tear. Hoping for the best he put it back where he had found it, thinking that the sheet might even have been torn when he took it.

Downstairs, small children battered at his father's unsteady legs, calling for apples and nuts like pups around a bitch's muzzle.

'God, I'm sorry. I forgot black about it.' His father was addressing his mother more than the children, though he would not look at her directly while he spoke. 'I met a man and we had some business to do. Look. I'm sorry. Isn't that enough for you?'

His mother closed her eyes and said she was going to bed.

'Look, I'm sorry. I'll go and get some apples and stuff now.'

His mother, getting slowly to her feet, said that the only places left open would be pubs, and hadn't he spent enough of the day in them.

His father said that he didn't want to fight, and told the children, who were silent now, to get ready for bed. They should have been asleep hours ago.

'But we were waiting for you.'

'Well it's bedtime now.'

Roy glared at his brothers and sisters, angry with them for not looking out of the window when he had gone to so much trouble for their sake.

'I'm not going to bed yet,' he said. 'I'm older so I should stay up longer.' But it didn't seem that either of his parents had heard him speak.

He woke late the next morning and, looking out across the garden in daylight and frost, felt embarrassment for the night before, and knew he would never mention it, not even to his mother. Neither of his parents were in the kitchen when he came down, but the door to the yard was open. Across the yard, his mother and father stood in the doorway of one of the stables. They didn't seem to hear him approach and stand behind them. Bell lay on the stable floor, dead still, with a large black pup stuck halfway inside her.

His father was saying, 'For God's sake, we can get another dog. I'll bury her before any of them see it.'

His mother said, 'No. That's enough. There'll be no more animals in this household. We can hardly look after ourselves. It's my fault she died. I won't go through this again.'

That evening his father was late home. He had forgotten the groceries, but had a black and tan puppy by way of compensation.

$\int$

THE STICKY CARPET

∫

My genitals withered the day that I left him, and soon afterwards I discovered food. At first it had seemed that there was no pleasure left in life, and no escape from the pain. The company of others compounded misery, and isolation fragmented what shreds were left of my sanity. The consumption of alcohol or other drugs changed maudlin thinking into morbid imaginings. If Tom had not locked himself out of the flat things might have ended badly. As far as I was concerned I was dead already, and it was only through inertia that I hadn't made it official.

It was a divided house and Tom had the upper half. At a quarter past six on a Tuesday evening in early October he rang my bell. It was the first conversation of more than three words I had had with him. He seemed distressed, apologised for disturbing me and asked if he could use my phone to call a locksmith.

'That seems a little extreme,' I said, as I showed him in. 'Haven't you got a spare set somewhere?'

He said that he had keys at the office, but wouldn't be able to get them until the morning. He made his predicament sound unreasonably hopeless.

'That's hardly the end of the world,' I said.

He smiled, embarrassed: a good smile. I made my offer without thinking, in response to the smile.

'You're welcome to stay here for the night. There's only

the sofa, but it's perfectly comfortable. Locksmiths cost a fortune these days.'

He made some token protestation out of politeness, and then offered to take me out to supper in return for my hospitality. The thought of going to a restaurant filled me with a dread that would be inexplicable to a stranger.

'Nonsense,' I said briskly. 'That won't be necessary.'

There was no food in the house, so I settled him in front of the television with a whiskey and said that I had to nip out for a minute, praying that the delicatessen in the next street might still be open.

It was nothing elaborate. I made him watercress soup and bacon sandwiches. Sometime between lighting the stove and watching him eat I realised that, for the first time in a long time, I had some sense of normality and a first stirring of sensual pleasure. The bacon was paper thin and smoked; the soup a clear deep green. The smell that filled the flat was enough to revive even my forgotten appetite.

'Sorry,' I said. 'It's nothing much.'

He attempted a look of scepticism, but failed on account of the effect the food was having on his features.

'Delicious,' he said.

The next day I made my own bread and the day after that it was chutney. Samples of both were sent upstairs to Tom. He accepted them with a refreshing greed, and an understandable awkwardness.

'Don't let it worry you,' I said. 'I spent a long time with someone who couldn't appreciate good things. We broke up not so long ago. If you take my food you are doing me a favour. Believe me.'

He asked me what my lover's name had been. It seemed an odd question.

'If I never say his name, someday I might forget it.'

I could see what Tom was thinking: that I was odd but harmless. That would have to do for the moment. After my previous experience, being thought harmless seemed like a compliment.

By the following week I was having friends round for supper. Some of them were people I hadn't seen for a long time. There is a limit to how much you can bore your friends with bruises and tears. Now, watching them eat my food left me nothing short of elated. I had made a perfect steak and kidney pudding. I was shaking with nerves as I cut it open and couldn't sit still until it had been tasted and its perfection declared. Tom was a guest also and I had been nervous about that, but my friends liked him. There was good conversation in the flat for the first time in ages.

Clarissa cornered me in the kitchen while I was fetching coffee and asked if Tom was my new man.

'Don't be such an old woman,' I said. 'He's just a neighbour. I don't even know if he's gay or straight.'

I took no notice of the knowing look she gave me. But she did say it was nice to see me being my old self again. Like someone risen from the dead she said. She was dipping her finger in the remains of the blackberry mousse.

'Delicious,' she said.

In time the two flats became a whole house again, by degrees, over the years. Tom and I were considered a couple. He ate my food and entertained my guests while I was in the kitchen. It was assumed, wrongly, that we shared a bed. He never made that demand and I was grateful for his forbearance. We had contentment and, looking about us, it seemed that our lives were better endowed than the lives of most others.

The name of that other person became dimmer, and thoughts of him less frequent. I had left him to save my life, or his, because it had come to a point where one of us would have killed the other. At first it had seemed that I hadn't a life worth saving, but in time I no longer thought about those things, only of the next meal. I worried about boudin blanc, not happiness. Food is very reliable. If something goes wrong it is entirely your own fault, and nothing is beyond salvation.

Inevitably, Tom sometimes suggested that we should go to a restaurant. That brought visions of all the restaurant meals in the past; of attempted conversation and long inebriated silences between a couple who were painfully in love and had nothing in common; of him being so drunk that he would vomit across the tablecloth and of me carrying him out under the pitying glare of the management. This was none of Tom's business.

I said, 'I have yet to eat at a restaurant where the food is as good as my own. It is a sinful waste of money. Don't you like what I cook for you?'

He would point out that I hadn't been to a restaurant for years; that things had improved.

'I read the papers. I know that the prices have gone up and the portions have got smaller and that the waiters now have ponytails. The food is still a matter of profit, not passion.'

If it had been anyone else but Tom we would have been fighting. He would have told me that it was a fat lot I knew about passion. He would have stormed out of the house and gone to a Burger King. But, being Tom, he put a forkful of gnocchetti into his mouth and said, 'Delicious.'

I did begin to wonder why he wasn't as hungry in the evenings as he used to be. Unbeknownst to me he was plotting; researching restaurants in his lunch breaks until he found one that would meet my standards. A week before his birthday I asked him what present he would like.

'The Sticky Carpet,' he said.

'The what?'

'I want you to let me take you to The Sticky Carpet.'

I thought it might be a play or a film or, perhaps, a particularly sordid nightclub.

'Fine,' I said. 'What time does it start? Should we have supper beforehand or should I make something for when we get home? I was going to do duck in red cabbage.'

'It is a restaurant,' he said. 'And you can't back out now. You've agreed. Birthdays are sacred.'

That week I cooked as I had never cooked before. My work was late and the editor complained, but some things are more important than reviewing obituaries for the *Telegraph*. If Tom was out to prove a point, then so could I. Whatever The Sticky Carpet might produce would pale in comparison to the meals which preceded it.

Tom was right. He had found the one restaurant in the country where the food was unimpeachable. Better than that, it was exciting. At first, I pretended not to be impressed.

'Anyone can buy good foie gras,' I said.

'Apparently,' Tom said, 'they make it themselves.'

For the second time in my life I had to admit defeat, but only to myself. And this defeat was full of pleasure. He had watched, amused, as I chose the most difficult and unlikely things (the foie gras was served on what the menu called 'Toasted Mango Brioche', which I was certain would be disgusting), and laughed when I had got to the stage of tasting things from his plate as well as my own.

When the bill was paid I had mellowed enough to say how nice it was not to have any washing-up to face. I was almost tempted to say something sentimental, but thought better of it.

By a quirk of architecture there was a door which connected the cloakroom with the kitchens, and this door had a window let into it, which I peered through as I put on my coat and waited for Tom to return from the lavatory. Chefs and cooks ran and shouted and stainless steel gleamed, and I was feeling pleased with myself that a ghost had been laid and that I had spent the entire evening without once thinking of him. There was something familiar about the man who was washing the saucepans and, as I took a second glance, he turned. It was him. Paunchier and at once more haggard, with that complexion like raw suet pastry that kitchen staff acquire, but him all the same.

I backed away from the door in case he saw me, afraid of what my mind would do next. I had lived for years with a terror of running into him again; of how the anger he had caused would manifest itself. Nothing happened. I felt nothing. I went and had another look. It was just a sad man, brought low by drink, in a demeaning job. There was a hand on my elbow. It was Tom.

'Are you ready?'

My hand brushed his as we left and it was like getting an electric shock. I began to shiver a little, knowing what was now inevitable. He asked me if I was all right, and I said it was just the cold.

When we got home he looked as though he was ready for bed, but I poured a drink for us, and we were at opposite ends of the sofa, and I was thinking that in all the things I had tasted over the years I had forgotten the taste of skin.

'Tom,' I said. 'Take your clothes off.'

He did it without question, and I looked at him for what seemed like a long time before anything happened, as though there might still be some way out of it. He waited, as he had always done, until I was ready. His body seemed extraordinary to me, and I thought if I touched it it might break. I hadn't the power to go any further on my own.

'Perhaps,' I said, 'you had better take mine off too. I don't think I'm able.'

He put his lips to mine and said, 'How's this?'

I was tempted to say that it was delicious, but that was a word for food, not lust.

∫

KENWOOD CHEF

∫

I never have, but I easily could sit down in a restaurant and have four puddings instead of the acceptable progression of starter, main course, pudding and coffee. It is part of a passion I shared with my mother while she was alive, which was for the first, and formative, half of my life. On expeditions to Waterford we would stop at a cake shop called The Green Bank on the way home, and buy a large box of meringues, éclairs and millefeuilles. Our intention would be to treat those siblings who had been left behind to a creamy tea, but by the time we reached the bridge over the Suir, which must have been all of six hundred yards beyond the cake shop, the box would be empty, and the two of us laughing at our own gluttony.

Not surprisingly, it was baking and not the rosary which provided the bonding in our house, and the nearest thing we had to a household god was a white and navy cake mixing machine with a stainless steel bowl. Or, at least, it was stainless steel to begin with, until my mother threw it at me in a fit of frustrated rage. The bowl missed me (as, no doubt, it was intended to) and bounced off the cobbles at my pony's heels. Thereafter it would not fit into the machine and had to be replaced by a ceramic affair, of which we were not so fond. I noticed the other day, in the basement of a department store, that Kenwood have returned to making their bowls in stainless steel, presumably to satisfy the mawkish nostalgia of the likes of me.

The day came when this overused machine, in the middle of mixing a batch of American frosting for a chocolate cake, gave out a whine and a puff of smoke and refused another revolution. The man who could mend it was sent for (we lived in the middle of nowhere and without a telephone, so don't ask me how), and arrived, and diagnosed death. It was a blow to us. My mother and I stood in the yard, watching the electrician's van drive off down the lane, thinking that an era was over. The machine was a hangover from more affluent days and there was no money to buy a new one.

The van we were watching passed another van just beyond the gate, the sight of which lifted our spirits somewhat. It had Lyon's Tea written on the side. My mother had been entering the Lyon's monthly draw in the hopes of winning a new car.

The unnecessarily handsome man from Lyon's asked my mother if she was Mrs Ronan, and she said that she was, and then he congratulated her. He opened the back of his van and took out a new Kenwood Chef, the same model as the recent mortality, although of a less attractive, brownish colour, and with a plastic bowl. I think, if I remember correctly, that we were too astonished to do anything but laugh.

If that story is less than interesting, it is because it is true in every detail, and therefore more of an anecdote than a story. Had I made it up I would have embellished it to make it more credible. I would not have relied so heavily on coincidence for a punchline; would have given it a soft malleable flesh of detail; would, perhaps, have given it meaning. For if a true story is anything it is meaningless, since, as any philosopher worth his salt will tell you, meaning is artificial. Someone once tried to convince me that there was a meaning behind that story and it was that God would provide whatever we truly needed. That person was too naive, too fixed on optimism for me to bother to explain to her that a new cake mixer was the last thing we needed. We could have mixed our cakes by hand. What we needed was a win in the sweepstakes, and a new floor in the sitting room where a stream seemed to have diverted itself beneath us and rotted all the joists. What we needed was for my father to go on the wagon. If God had nothing better to do than organise coincidental cake mixers then the universe was a mad, diseased place and there was no hope for us at all.

That was an anecdote, and this is a story to make up for it. It concerns, as a lot of stories do, the last person with whom the author had the misfortune to be emotionally entangled. I have just reached the stage when I can write stories about her, which will precede the stage when I realise that I have no regrets (it was awful, but at least I came out of it with the material for a few stories), which will be a time of danger, for then I will be happy enough in my single state to be unaware of the traps that the next person is setting for me. At the moment I am still miserable enough to be ineligible. No one in their right mind asks me for my telephone number the morning after, and I cannot ask for theirs, knowing that I will sound too eager.

We used to see each other in a club we both went to, and often we would chill together, in a companionable way, between bouts of dancing, making salacious remarks about the legs of men which passed at face level, for we would sit on the floor with our water bottles and our chewing gum and cigarettes. Her name, for the purposes of this story, was Olivia. Mine might as well remain what it is. What is the point, and who am I kidding, if I call myself Adam, Hugh, John or Jody?

So, early on, Olivia and I discovered we had a lot in common. We both went for the same type; both drooled over tall, lean sandy-haired men with sad eyes and large knuckles.

'What my mother,' I remarked, 'would have called Hungry Looking. It was, I think, the highest accolade to physical beauty in her vocabulary.'

Olivia said that she would like to have met my mother.

That was before we were anything more than friends, but I remember thinking even then that the person Olivia would have liked to have met was not my mother, but my version of her. Just as well, really, that the woman was dead and in no position to contradict the glowing portrait I liked to present.

She was not the first woman I had fallen in love with, but I suspect she will be the last. Falling in love is such a hopeless business that you might as well be hung for a sheep as a lamb; might as well go the whole hog and do it with a dream beefcake. There's no real point in loving someone who is sensitive and intelligent and not your physical ideal. In love we are all levelled to become the same screaming irrational monsters. To fall in love with someone you can laugh with is a waste of a potentially good friend. There's sod all to laugh about in love, and the times you do laugh will be drowned out by the times you shriek your hatred. You might as well take up with someone with whom you can have decent sex between the battles, so that the entire exercise isn't a waste. Save the sensitive souls for friendship. You can't have too many friends to bore with your tragedy when things go wrong in love. And they will.

'Olivia,' I said, as I lay in her arms in the aftermath of our first consummation, 'am I drunk or is there something happening here?'

She said that she had been afraid to say anything in case she was imagining it. Having sex with a gay man was one thing, but thinking yourself to be falling in love with him was not the most sensible move in a girl's amorous career.

'Oh dear God,' I said. 'I'm so ashamed. What am I going to tell my friends?' And we had to bite on the same pillow to stop ourselves being sick with laughter.

She asked me what my mother had looked like.

'Why are you so obsessed with my mother?'

She denied that she was.

'Yes you are. You never ask about my father, my brothers, sisters, aunts and cousins. You assume that because I'm queer I've got a thing about my mother. I don't. She was a good woman. I liked her. She died. I miss her. She doesn't hold the key to the dark recesses of my soul or anything.'

Olivia sulked after that conversation. It was our first disagreement. We should have split up then. Be faithful and cleave unto her until the first sulk, and then buy yourself a new pair of shoes and get down the club. There's plenty more who'll be prepared to smile for a fortnight.

And then things went along the predictable course that affairs take, regardless of the sexes of the participants. We shopped, fought, made up, frustrated each other sexually, talked about needing more time together and more time apart in practically the same breath, lied a lot about the need for honesty and weeded through each other's friends until we had no one left to talk to but ourselves. This took four and a half months, which doesn't sound like a long time, but is a fairly big chunk of the short and brutal life that I intend to live.

It ended, I think, the day we were walking through the basement of a department store, being seriously domestically concerned. We must have thought that if we behaved like old married people we could ignore the fact that we were falling apart. By doing things that were no fun at all we could overcome the fact that things were no fun any more. We bickered, because I wanted to spend a lot of money on a toaster that was beautiful while she was inclined towards the cheap one with the wheatsheaf stencilled on the side. She said it was only a toaster. What did it matter what it looked like?

'You don't understand, do you? What is the point of having anything at all unless it is a pleasure to look at? I suppose next you'll want me to dress in a shell suit.'

And so forth.

Out of the corner of my eye I saw the navy and white cake mixer with the stainless steel bowl and, for some reason, started to walk towards it. She followed, talking at my elbow, and it took her some time to realise that I wasn't answering. She must have looked up at my face. She must have seen that it was wet, and I could hear her asking what the matter was, but as though she was in another room. The stainless steel bowl bounced on the cobbles of the yard. I had refused to let my brother ride my pony. He was ham-fisted. He would, in my opinion, have damaged the pony's mouth; have undone all my schooling. I was right, and my mother knew it, but she must have thought that some things were more important than a pony's schooling. My chest burned with rage, and still I knew that her rage was worse. Love her children as she might, she couldn't make them love each other.

I realised then that there was no way of loving without shouting, and I knew that I couldn't stand any more shouting; could do more easily without love. I pulled out my shirt tail to wipe away the snot and tears, and tried to focus on where Olivia was standing. For the first time in weeks she seemed rather beautiful: her eyebrows crossed in concern, her mouth open in shock, her cheeks red with embarrassment.

'I don't want to love you any more,' I said. 'It may take a while, but I can learn not to love. I think the less you love, the happier you can be.'

I remember my mother who, given her circumstances, was the happiest woman alive, saying once that only the dead were happy. She felt that she could trust her children with such confidences.

∫

THE LAST INNOCENCE OF SIMEON

$\int$

Exterior, garden, day. What more could you ask for? Well, granted there was sunshine through the high trees on the boundary and the hollowness of birdsong from within the hedges, and the lane away from the garden had never seemed longer or greener, or more as though it led somewhere and not just to the road to the town. And, Mrs Doyle, thinking herself alone, sat near some bearded irises she was tiring of, and wept for a while.

No, she thought. Mourning, not weeping.

She laughed at herself then, for reaching the age that she had without losing an adolescent capacity for self-dramatisation; and she told herself not to be such an old woman, and felt beside her for her secateurs and string, thinking, because she believed it to be so, that business might clear her mind; and she chanced, as her hand closed on the softness of the string ball, to glance down the longer, greener lane, down to where parts of the felled tree lay across it, still.

She thought of Simeon now, and smiled, and noticed the heat of the climbing sun on her face.

Not far away and well within walking distance, by field or the road depending on the weather, Simeon had other things on his mind, shaving cream over half his face, and a visitor at an unreasonable hour for visitors. To make matters worse, the visitor was screaming at him in a voice devoid entirely of reason, and shaking out her hair as if to emphasise that there was madness in her anger. Simeon (or Simmy, as those who had known him since childhood thought of him, though because he had made little progress beyond the geographical bounds of that childhood the diminutive maintained a currency at an age when something a little more dignified might have been called for) continued his shaving; his mirror propped on the kitchen dresser; his hands, beautiful for their enormity alone, moving slowly to delay the moment when he would have to turn and face the harridan who had chosen to love him, whom he had once chosen to be loved by.

'Leave it so. Leave it so, will you? Don't be always shouting at me.'

'I think,' she said, 'I have the right.' Would it be unfair to suggest that she spoke with a certain coldness? Though not yet the mistress of her art, she knew something of the craft of control.

She watched the mirror, hiding her love as his face was uncovered from the shaving cream.

The more I think about it, the more I think it had something to do with the curve of his mouth. In other respects he was immaculate, handsome beyond doubt; but it was the mouth which made you think that there was more to him, more than the cipher that any square-chinned blue-eyed boy can be.

'This place is disgusting. A pig wouldn't live in it.' She kicked at the pile of hardened chicken crap on the tiles beneath the one chair.

'Clean it, so. If you're that worried about it.'

He had turned, and was facing her, square on. Now that his jaw was clean he felt an unwarranted courage in the face of her anger.

'Nobody asked you to come around at this hour of the morning and I still above in the bed. Nobody asked you to folly me around the house screaming like you have two heads on you. I was going to be picking you up at the usual time tonight but, as it is, maybe I've had enough of you for the day. Now, if you don't mind, I have work to be going to.'

It caught her unawares, to be spoken to, with authority, from a quarter where authority had been so far dormant. It made her want to explain herself, an impulse as alien to her as she had thought authority to be to Simmy. She wanted to tell him how she had woken up with such a happiness, and the freshness of early summer and early morning outside the window, and she had thought of him, and come along, late though it would make her for work, just to see his face, maybe kiss him good morning, maybe tickle him as he lay in the bed, maybe tell him of her happiness.

She would have told him all that except that she couldn't now pinpoint the moment, between her entering the house and his opening his eyes, that her euphoria had changed to a black, uncontrollable anger; couldn't decide whether it had been caused by the filthy state of the place, or the smell of beer on his morning breath, or the slow, autistic complacency with which he woke. It might have been – it probably was – the sight of him alone in a big bed, apparently contented even though she was absent from it. It might have had something to do with – and probably had – the big smile on his sleeping face, and her not knowing what or whom it was that he was dreaming of.

And, as had been intended, she was dumbfounded by the last thing he had said.

'Work?' she said. 'Where?'

'That got you.'

He was smiling, and though it could have been a smile of triumph, his smile was gentle on her. Now that she had stopped her screaming he had nothing against her at all.

'I'm felling a tree for Mrs Doyle beyond. I have the back broke of it yesterday, and I'll finish clearing it today.'

'How much is she giving you?' She could have bitten

her tongue for the mean question as soon as she had asked it.

'Enough.'

He turned his shoulder on her and left the house in his shirtsleeves, with her looking after him; with her deciding that she would get the morning off work and clean his house for him, and say nothing about it afterwards; with her wondering how it was that she loved him most in his absence.

He went by the fields, through grass as thick and wet as seaweed, and before Mrs Doyle came into view he could hear the scraping and clicking and swearing of her working her garden. He hung on the gate so as not to startle her, until she had seen him out of the corner of her eye.

'Is it breakfast time already?' she asked.

When he thought about it in the years to come, it seemed to him that she had said many extraordinary things that day, but he distrusted the memory, thinking that he had amalgamated in his mind things she must have said to him over the years, condensing them to one, significant, lengthy and broken conversation over the making of firewood and the tidying of a summer garden.

'How is Maggie keeping?' she asked.

'You know yourself.'

'That bad?'

'As bad as that.'

'The first one is always the greatest pain in the backside.'

'The first what?'

'The first person you let fall in love with you. Let that be a lesson to you, when you find yourself in the same condition. It's no picnic.'

She had a wry smile on her, and he was sniggering, and they felt, for some reason, that they understood each other.

'Mourning, not weeping,' she said, at another time,

snatching the phrase back from earlier in the morning, and muttering it as though she were alone, or as though they had taken drink, or as though she had nothing left to lose, or as though she were in no danger of losing it to him.

'Mourning?'

'Not the way you'd think. Not for the dead, any of them. For the things I can't have; thought I would surely have by now and know now I never will have. It's hard to reconcile being so selfish and hiding the selfishness with a lifetime of manners, and still not always getting your own way.'

'I know.'

'Times I want to bulldoze this garden. Will you look at it? All flowers and at the highest pitch of prettiness, and all it stands for is that it's the only thing I could do. Times I think it's pathetic, the delight I get. Do you know, the most irritating thing anyone ever said to me?'

'That must have been a powerful one.'

'You can't have everything.' I was six and it was a nun, and I remember thinking then, even then, and I've thought it all the time since, why not? No one has ever proved that you can't have everything. Because something has never been done before does not make it impossible. There will, mark my words, be, one day, a happy member of this species who is still in possession of his sanity.'

'Sounds good to me.'

'Don't kid yourself,' she said. 'It won't happen by chance.'

Sometime in the heat of the afternoon, with tea and melting chocolate-covered biscuits, and Simmy stripped to the waist, as though he were unconscious that it might be unfair to show such a body to someone who could not possess it, he asked Mrs Doyle what had ended the bench.

To her, it was like changing the subject, because she had been looking at him so critically that he must have been aware of it. (She had been running her eye up and down the skin and the muscle and thinking: that is all he thinks there is to it; just that face and that body and he thinks there need be no more to him; as complacent as a bull in a field; as if there was something wrong with thinking and something worse with making a life for yourself.) She had, at the moment of his question, been about to say something irritable.

'Bench?' she said.

'It was there yesterday. We sat on it for the tea.'

Marks were on the ground where the bench feet had stood for decades; there was a palpable absence in Simmy's line of sight. Mrs Doyle kept looking, level, at him.

'A tinker offered me good money for it, and I took it.'

'For God's sake.'

'For God's sake, what?'

'You're paying me over the odds for cutting the wood as it is.'

'I'll pay you whatever the notion takes me to pay you and you won't pretend you don't want it.'

'Wanting is one thing and fair is another, and besides, I liked the bench.'

'You can save sentimentality for your old age, when you have nothing better to do with your mind.' She made a grimace of self-mockery, perhaps because their talk had become too much like fighting, and she knew that if she made him angry she would never get him to do what she wanted of him: it being easier to lead a bull than drive one.

The face she made reassured him, and while his guard was down she said, 'I'm always surprised, when I think about it, to find you staying in this place, with nothing to keep you. If you're not careful you'll wake up old one of these days. Or, at least, too old to do anything about it.'

'About what?' He was looking at her with a discomfort which amounted to fear, and it wasn't just that the tone of their talk was more serious than anything between them might warrant.

When she saw how she had discomfited him she felt herself to be on the right track, and proceeded.

'I think you know. At least I'm not prepared to be the first of us to mention a word that describes it. That will have to be your own doing, in your own time. We are talking about the thing you least want us to be talking about. The thing that has you shivering in the heat, now.'

'There are some things you don't talk about.' He said that with the outraged modesty of a child who has been surprised on the lavatory.

'If that is how you feel, perhaps you have to find a place where you're not afraid to talk about things.'

Now there was a coldness between them; one that had been far from her intentions. He went back to what was left of the tree, where he worked with a savagery that made you think the muscles of his arms would explode.

She went into the house and watched him from a window, telling herself that she should not be astonished by his anger. The animal you rescue is not to know that you are trying to help it. From the back of her mind, at the same time, came the accusation that she was doing this thing more for herself than for him; that she was only salving her conscience for having let another man, and one she loved more, live and die, before she thought these things, let alone said them.

Thinking too that she had said, had assumed, too much; knowing at the same time that she had assumed correctly and not said enough.

Evening, and the wood stacked precisely, and the noise of the chainsaw finished with and the axes and wedges back in the shed, and only a scattering of sawdust by the stump of the tree, and bits of it lodged in Simeon's eyebrows and hair, and him smiling in the first crowd of midges, with satisfaction, you would think, for the work finished. Smiling, perhaps, in hopes of returning to a frame of mind he thought he had had earlier in the day; to conversations that were easy, knowing and bantering, and the subtexts of which were not his own, barely acknowledged, can of worms. (Best left unopened, he thought, pulling the smile tighter, until he was almost laughing with the effort of it.)

Mrs Doyle was standing, with her head to one side, looking at him, and with a sudden shame he cast about him for his shirt, brushing wood dust from his nipples as if he were contaminated.

She smiled, able to read what was printed in lines across his forehead: she cannot know, she's only guessing, and even so there's no way she can have guessed that, the last thing anyone would guess of me, since I'm not convinced of it myself, since it isn't true, not really.

'That's lovely now,' she said.

'I made it as tidy as I could.'

'A work of art,' she said. 'You're very neat.'

'Thanks.' His smile now was one of genuine relief. The subject which had threatened earlier seemed firmly closed again. 'I'd better be off home to the bath. I said I'd take Maggie out. She'll eat me if I'm late.'

'Come in the house for your wages first.'

He followed her, shambling, as though he suspected a trap. Once they were inside the kitchen he was aware of the pungent smell of himself, fresh enough to be more provocative than unpleasant. There were two envelopes lying on the long table. He picked at his fingernails.

She picked up both the envelopes and handed him one. The other she placed on the dresser, propped before a small pale yellow jug. It had his full name written on it.

'I'm leaving that there,' she said, 'and it's yours whenever you want it. You can, of course, do what you like with it, but it's enough for the boat and to see you through for a week or two until you find yourself a job. You could, I suppose, buy a gimcrack engagement ring for the Hanlon girl with it. She'd like that.'

She saw that he was staring at the floor and that his body was rocking, unstable.

She said, 'I'm sorry for the things I said earlier, but I had to do this, for my own sake. Eddie Doyle was like you and I watched him rot his life out married to me. The signs were there, but I never saw them till after he was dead. You can see nothing if you love someone enough. These days I see too much, including you for what you are. And you won't thank me for it. But the times are different now, and if you go away you'll find there's nothing wrong with what you are; it's only this place and others like it. Anyway, the money's yours and you're not to say anything. Not a word. The back door, as you know, is always open, whenever you're ready to take it.'

He wished for the floor to open and swallow him; was surprised he had the strength to turn and leave the house.

She said, in his wake, 'We'll all have to mourn, one of the days. But I'd rather see you mourning for a full life than an empty one.'

He began to walk quickly, into the dew, trying to outpace the words that came after him, blind in his fear and thinking that this must be the end of everything, calling her a bitch, twice, to every pace he took.

∫

DUCK IN RED CABBAGE

∫

Luke was someone they hardly knew at all. Because they
both liked him, this unfamiliarity was, to some extent,
deliberate. And because he liked both of them, or seemed
to, and they did not have many friends like that, or know
many people who were unaware of their history. Almost
everyone, at one time or another, had been forced to
take sides, and there were times when the only people
who seemed to think that Mark and John should stay
together were themselves. That was the value of Luke: by
keeping him at a distance they could have one friend whose
company was pleasurable and nothing more. They could
pretend, when they saw him, that they had ordinary lives.

They knew him from the Fridge and for a long time they
knew him only as the bear. Every Saturday night he would
be in the same corner, on the left-hand side, below where
their dealer stood. The bear would always be the one beside
you when your E came up too fiercely and you started to
hyperventilate, his hand massaging the back of your neck,
his water bottle ready for small sips, his voice reminding you
to breathe slowly, his body, big and downy, in place for you
to drape yourself around it when things got mongified and
your own legs turned to sponge and you needed to be held
for a moment, or for a long time, or when time had ceased
to be fathomable and you needed anchorage.

They must have exchanged telephone numbers with the

bear twice or three times, over coffee at McDonald's, on those painful Sunday mornings, with the Brixton sun shrieking in the windows; while you ground your teeth and stared at the zoo of queens around you; hoping that you didn't look as bad as all the other tripped-out, clubbed-out death's-heads: knowing well you probably did; wondering if you had the money, in wet, crumpled denominations, to buy the energy to go on to Trade and make a weekend of it; knowing that you'd rather be home in bed, coming down gently (in the case of Mark and John, those come-downs being some of the few gentle times between them, wrapped on each other with every limb and separated only by the skin of chemical sweat and the puerile, chemical wish that it could always be this way). And though numbers would always be exchanged, scribbled with borrowed eye pencil on the back of a sugar packet, they were easy to lose, or maybe they just melted in the cold sweat of your back pocket in the cab, because it was a long time before the phone rang and John answered it and the bear was on the other end, holding an undissolved sugar packet in his hand, and by that time John and Mark had almost come to the end of the madness that tethered them.

'Luke?'

'From the Fridge. Luke and Matthew.'

'The bear?' John guessed. The voice was not the same now that neither of them was under the influence of drugs.

The bear laughed.

You think you sound normal: that you are still in control; that someone would have to know you well to suspect that something was wrong. It may have been that the bear heard a desperation in John's voice, or it may have been that John, in desperation, imagined the bear's concern, but, in either case, when John was asked how he was, the question sounded so solicitous that he almost answered it honestly.

He said that he was fine.

Then the bear asked how Mark was. Though Mark would have favoured an elaborate lie in response to this (had, indeed, instructed him to lie if anyone asked, saying it was nobody's business but their own), John was, to tell the truth, a slow and unnatural liar, and his stock of ready-made lies had already been exhausted by his last utterance. There was no time to prepare and rehearse a new lie, and so nothing he could do in this case but let slip the truth; trying, nonetheless, to spike it with levity, even if the breath which carried the words out felt like the first breath in living memory.

'He isn't here. I finally got him into a clinic this afternoon. He should be out of circulation for a few weeks.'

'Drink?'

'How did you know?'

'It was fairly obvious.'

That remark made John feel foolish. It had taken him three months of living with the man before he had worked out that there was a problem. And another six months to persuade Mark that there might be one. Now, a virtual stranger could see, straight away, that which had been hidden from him for so long, by sociability, by hedonism and murmured assurances couched in love.

'How are you doing?' The bear spoke as if there had been a long silence on John's part. Perhaps there had been.

'Fine.'

'Do you need to talk?'

It was hard enough just holding a telephone conversation. Do you know the feeling that if you start to talk you will lose everything? Lose it, as they say.

'No. No, it's fine. You just called at a bad moment.'

Thinking that, for God's sake, you hardly knew the man. How could you begin to explain it to him, when you didn't have the courage to talk about it to your friends any more? And wouldn't the bear just say what they all said? Get out, while you're still alive. And wouldn't Mark make that face that frightened you and say that it was nobody's business but our own, but his own. He had once said that it was none of your business either. You didn't understand.

You would be better to wait, and give the clinic a chance. Give Mark a chance. Better, much better not to talk about it until the rosy times ahead, after the cure.

'Are you still there?'

Of course you were still there. You were just thinking of duck in red cabbage. It had just struck you that that was what you would make for the homecoming supper. It could be done the day before. You could pick him up in the morning, and the two of you could spend the day driving in the countryside. It would, of course, be fine weather. Fine views to look at from the safety of the other side of the cure. Now was a time to be borne with gritted teeth. Soon to be forgotten in the light of the future.

'Yes. Sorry.'

'There's nothing to be sorry for. Look, if you want to talk – not necessarily now, but anytime – just give me a ring and come round.' The bear gave John his number and address. 'Even if it's the middle of the night. It doesn't matter.'

Say thanks, but not feeling grateful; wondering instead why the bear was talking to you as though it was you who had the problem. The problem was in the clinic, being solved.

Something light to start with. You needed to leave plenty of room for a dish like duck in red cabbage. A salad of bitter leaves and mango perhaps. Marinade a raw leek in balsamic vinegar for the dressing. Florence fennel. Cape gooseberries?

'Luke?' he said. 'Sorry.'

'For what?'

'I think I'm being a bit off-hand.'

'No, you aren't. And if you are I don't think it's beyond understanding. Look, if you aren't sure about being on your own while he's away, there's a spare bed here. Matthew and I will look after you.'

'No. I mean I have to be here. Where he thinks I am. It's fine. Sorry. I mean thanks. Look, I can't do this. I can't afford to crack up now. He needs one of us to stay sane.'

That day, into which events were crowded with the gregariousness of number 23 buses; into which the sordid past and glimmering future should have dovetailed; the day it seemed, at every hour, that there was a new and different possibility for the life ahead – but you should have known that change won't root itself in such a skein of drama, and that revolution is a slow turn (and nothing takes as long as watching for the dawn) and we only realise how different things are after they have become so – that was the day that Mark Edward Baker had the self-discipline to last five hours in a clinic after it had taken half a year to persuade him to enter it.

And all he could say was, 'Do you think I'm proud of it?'

And that was supposed to be a rhetorical question.

He had five hours in the clinic and six hours in the pub, working up the courage to come home (or maybe just getting drunk).

He looked so afraid of you as he fell through the door that you knew what was likely to come next. You hoped (if hope is something you can feel at a moment of complete hopelessness, when you have the physical sensation of fall-ing freely towards the centre of the earth, when everything around you is suspended, as at the moment of hearing of a death when you can only hope – there, hope again – that this, in fact, is not happening), you prayed that he might fall unconscious before his fists began to flail, and that he might stay unconscious until the morning, when he would be too ill to do anything but apologise.

It is a bad sign when he can't look you in the eye, at first, and then, when things are settled in his mind, can look you hard in the eye as though the whole thing was your fault, and your fault alone.

What sort of sign is it when you are marking the escape routes before the row has even started?

Is it a good sign that you are leaving now, before you have said a single word?

There wasn't time to construct a plan based on any logic. The hours since the bear had phoned John, and made him promise to come round if he needed to, had been collapsed into a sleep that seemed minutes long. Exhausted by the near-misses of that conversation, John had fallen asleep on the sofa, the envelope, with the bear's address on it, still, for some reason, in his hand. He had woken to the sound of the key in the lock, to the sight of Mark falling through the door, to the sensation that everything was lost and there was nothing more he could do.

It was lucky for him that the night was balmy, since he hadn't even taken the time to think to put on a coat before leaving. He held himself in numbness while waiting at the mini-cab office and then, once he was in the passenger seat of the cab, he began to feel the dreadful creeping of water from his eyes. At least it was dark and he was a noiseless weeper. He could, had he the energy, have made it seem like hayfever. He could, if he had really cared what cab drivers thought (and this was not the first one in whose company he had sniffled), have walked.

The bear opened the door, and said, 'I thought I'd be seeing you before the night was out.'

That did it: ten minutes before he could say anything at all and then he could only say he was sorry, and in a voice strangled from howling. And then tried to light a cigarette, to gain some control, over his breathing, if nothing else.

Matthew took the cigarette from his shaking hands and lit it for him and handed it back. He looked up, and saw Matthew to his left and the bear to his right, and the four arms stretched to him; the hands on his shoulders and knees; the comfort of men. He said he was sorry.

The bear said that if he said that again he'd be thrown out.

They rolled a joint, a strong one, and made you smoke the whole thing yourself, and one of them rubbed your feet and the other massaged your shoulders, and they let you blether, haver, lapse back into your apologies, and they said little, nothing that was not of use, until you felt you didn't know what but something you were not afraid of feeling, for a change.

Afraid of talking complete nonsense and boring them shitless, you pull yourself back to the beginning of things, to the time you met Mark, and you recount every germane detail that has led to this (there are surprisingly few); to your sitting on the bear's hearthrug, wrecked. Because this feels as though it might be the end, the whole thing has become, in some ways, a story. The plot is clear; clearing by the minute; has much to do with your own stupidity; with your arrogance in thinking that you could save a soul by loving it. You are not, the bear tells you, the Redeemer.

That is not, the bear tells you, a failure.

Talk the disjointed story until the eyes close of their own volition. Stoned and drained, John hardly knew that the bear and Matthew had put him to bed.

Thinking about it afterwards, it must have been a noise that woke him up, but by the time he was conscious there was only the near-silence of a high bedroom in South London at 4.13 in the morning by one of those digital clocks that lit up the bedside with a sickly glow. He thought, maybe, he could hear whispering.

At first it was strange to wake alone, with no bare shoulder beside you to kiss in that form of affection best reserved for the sleeping. Then he remembered that Mark was in the clinic, and that was why he was alone, and he

• Handsome Men Are Slightly Sunburnt

smiled at the rosy future. Then his eyes focused and he
knew himself to be in a strange bed and a strange house,
and he remembered the last time he had woken, and the
reality.

He was aware that his breath was shortening with panic;
that an instinct for flight was taking him over. He tried to
fight this desire to run and hide, with common sense, by
reminding himself that he had run; that he was hiding; that
Mark would never think of looking for him here. When
the panic did not subside he did not have the presence of
mind to conclude that it was not for his own safety he was
panicking.

He thought he could hear whispering that was a little
fierce.

He tried to remember the sound of the bear's voice; the
sound advice; the counsel that matched the counsel of
every other sane person he had spoken to. He remembered,
instead, the sound of his own voice, telling the bear and
Matthew that the camel's back was broken; that there was
no hope left; that if he went back this time he might as well
be dead.

He thought he heard a scream.

For half an hour he lay paralysed while they fought
below him. The bear and Matthew, in voices that were
recognisable but not like their own, in a passion of lovers'
hatred that forgot his presence in the room above them. It
took the whole of the thirty minutes for the idea he had
been waiting for to come to him.

He thought: 'If I have to deal with this sort of shit anyway,
I've got my own, at home, to deal with.'

In the minutes of dressing there was new hope. He hadn't,
after all, given Mark a chance to explain himself. And if he
went back now, it wouldn't look too bad. It might seem
as though he had only been out to clear his head, not as
though there had been an abandonment. The ferocity he
could hear below him made him think that, maybe, ferocity

was the price you paid for a bare shoulder to kiss when you woke at 4.13 in the morning.

Pre-dawn South London, imbued with unearthly bird-song that echoed on the yellow brick, and the sound of your own footfalls as loud as anything, for once. And there was no reason not to think of an excuse to make the duck in red cabbage anyway. You cooked the duck and the cabbage separately at first: the cabbage chopped fine, with an onion, several apples, cloves, a lemon, sugar, salt, pepper, red wine, water, cider vinegar; covered and put in the oven for a long, slow time. When it was done you removed it and turned the oven up and blasted the duck, having stuffed it with chopped Toulouse sausages. Then you added the meat to the cabbage and returned it to a slow oven, while you made a sauce with the juices and some good, bitter marmalade. This, you added also. A proper purée of potatoes, made with crème fraîche and involving a fair amount of forkwork went well with it. A pudding made of poached apricots and ricotta perhaps.

The clear sound of your footfalls and a good kitchen fantasy will carry you a long way without you realising it. And at the end of it he will be asleep across the bed, unaware of whether you have been gone for an hour or six, and you kiss the bare shoulder as you creep beside him and you try not to think of anything but the finer details of the apricot and ricotta pudding. And you tell yourself that, the way things are, they can only get better.

∫

THE LAST INNOCENCE OF SIMEON

∫

Interior, château, twilight. Thinking that, no matter how bad things got, one seemed to stumble from one idyll to another, in sensual terms at least. The milk-yellow stone of the fireplace deepening between one glance and the next; the distant ceiling fading, and then blacked out by the lighting of the lamps; the sparse conversation and elongated breathing of a kind of contentment that came with comfort and an indulged palate; the faint hope that the children would settle in strange surroundings and that the last had been seen of them until morning; the mixed scents of itea and cestrum groping a way through the open door, a conjunction of smells odd enough to be without association; the luxury of a clear subconscious; the occasional small cold breeze from the direction of the same doorway, just enough to keep you this side of dozing.

'What exactly is it that you do?'

There was a level on which Simeon enjoyed being asked that question. He liked to make a game of the answer, prevaricating as though he were being discreet and not ashamed. He was not, he told himself emphatically, ashamed. He was happy about what he did: his unhappiness lay in other people's perception of his job.

'I organise things.'

'What sort of things?'

There was something in the persistence of his interlocutor

which had nothing to do with curiosity. Simeon raised a hand to shade his eyes from the pale orange cast of the nearest lamp, and had a proper look. The upper half of the face was in shade; the lower half a strong chin of some rotundity, and one of those inward-facing mouths. A long bony hand lay nearby, detached, by a trick of the light.

'Well, I suppose I'm a sort of enabler.'

'What's that supposed to mean?'

He had been right about the tone of his questioner's voice. If it was provocative there was also an element of flirtatiousness. Simeon cast a quick, automatic, almost imperceptible glance in the direction of Jane. The mother of his children had the tip of her thumb in her mouth, her head bent over one of her hard-backed novels, in a daze of reading. At the other end of the sofa which she occupied, their host snoozed; layers of sleek dog in his lap.

'You could say that the parameters of my work are, loosely, perhaps ultimately, lifestyle investment.'

'You could say that you were an estate agent.' Their host, evidently, had not been asleep after all. Having spoken, he roused himself, sending rolls of dog tumbling to the floor. The cynical boom of his voice had caused Jane to look from her book to her watch.

'I'm for bed,' she said. 'Darling?'

Simeon was aware, without looking, of the way in which the questioner must be smiling. This was no time to retreat; this was no taste to leave in the mouth of another.

'I'll be up soon,' he said.

Soon enough, he thought. He set himself the task of remembering the other man's name. Christopher.

When the two men were alone Christopher got up to close the door into the garden.

'I'm having another drink,' he said. 'I don't know about you.'

Simeon said, 'Whiskey.' It was obvious now in which direction things were heading. He became aware of how he was sitting; that his legs were spread a little further than relaxation might call for.

Christopher handed him a glass that was a drip wet on the outside, the pads of their middle fingers touching as the handover was made. Simeon hoped that his shiver would not be taken for the nervousness it was.

'I don't blame you, really.' Christopher looked him straight in the eye while speaking. 'It must be bad enough to be an estate agent without having to tell people about it.'

Christopher was leaning against the edge of a table, his arms over his chest. He had, Simeon noticed, the sort of thighs that would look good folded, knee to shoulder. Simeon pulled a cushion into his lap, as though to fiddle idly with the tassles. Meanwhile, he laughed at the last thing Christopher had said.

'And so what do you do?' Simeon thought he might as well get that one out of the way.

'I manage campaigns for Friends of the Earth.'

Simeon said that that must be interesting, in a tone of voice which implied that they didn't have to talk about it.

The high windows were silvering. They became notice-able in the conversational hiatus, and served as a way out of it.

Simeon said, 'The moon is up.'

Christopher said, 'Shall we go for a walk?'

The bench was surrounded on three sides by sharp-cornered yew, silver and blackened in the brightness of the moon. The change of light made a difference, it seemed, to everything: the garden monochromatically formalised; Christopher's face given a cast that made him familiar.

'You remind me of someone.'

There seemed no point, once it was said, in having said it. The association faded as soon as it was confessed, as the memory of a dream will fade as soon as a breakfast companion has been bored by the telling of it.

'Who?'

'No one you'd know.'

Simeon became aware of the smell of the other man, and wondered for a moment why he had not noticed it before, and then realised how illogical it was to wonder such a thing, because it was only a minute or so since he had stretched himself out flat on his back the length of the bench and rested his head on Christopher's lap. It was a smell that was not entirely of man: there was an odd taint of aniseed in it, and Simeon wondered if it was the soap he used, or whether it was natural to him.

Christopher, playing with Simeon's fringe, said, 'You don't sound very Irish.'

'Don't I? Would you rather I did?' It was an effort to make the words come out in a discernible pattern; to make sounds that were anything more than the grunts of desperation that were lining up at his throat.

The noise, when it was released, was stifled because Christopher's mouth closed on his at the same moment that Christopher's hand went down the flat of his stomach and wound itself round his erection.

'That's some fucking monster you've got there.'

For the first time Christopher's tone was not one of accusing banter, as though he had finally found something admirable in Simeon.

Simeon opened his eyes. The face was eight inches from his, and smiling, and seemingly sinister viewed from below and in the half-light. Not knowing how to take the compliment, Simeon said, 'It's not my fault.'

'Do you always shake this much?'

'I don't know.' Simeon had to stop himself and think about what to say next. This was not the moment to admit that he had never done this before. 'Yes,' he said, 'I suppose so.' As if to change the subject he buried his face in the folds of the other man's flies.

The next words spoken were said by Christopher.

'That was an Irish groan if ever I heard one. You sound much more Irish when you're coming.'

There were bats flashing overhead.

'Why do your balls smell of aniseed?' Simeon sniffed closer to reassure himself that his question was justified.

'Do they?'

From the corner of his eye Simeon became aware of the appearance of a yellow light. He looked towards the silhouette of the château and watched the lighted window until it became dark again. Someone using a bathroom, obviously. He worried that it was Jane; that she had woken, had missed him, had noticed how late it had become. He wondered idly, academically, what to do now about Jane: whether one night of felicity had cancelled out eight years of fidelity; whether this was something he just needed to do every eight years, or whether he was debauched now, corrupted; whether there was no turning back once a lifetime's resolve had fissured.

He pulled himself closer, pushed his face into the smell of aniseed and the slick flaccid tangle, until breathing became mercifully difficult, until a new tumescence pushed him into renewed activity.

Like an unwilling and unbelieving parachutist clinging to the door jamb of an aeroplane, those of us who are genuinely innocent will cling to the last remnant of that innocence; will cling even to the memory of how that door jamb felt in our hand although we are already tumbling through the void, towards freedom.

It was mid-afternoon, after a morning of disconnection, before Simeon had the chance to be alone with Christopher. He hadn't gone to bed until nearly dawn, and Jane had sleepily wrapped herself around him, had sleepily asked him the time, had sleepily accepted his denial of knowledge of the time, had sleepily submitted to his ferocious lovemaking and, once aroused, had thrown herself open to him with an enthusiasm and a pleasure and an abandonment that only, somehow, made things worse. It had been a morning of responding to the children in the sort of snappish tones that let them know this was not a time for the sort of parent-child bonding recommended by the textbooks. It had been a morning of keeping tight hold of any inanimate object that came to hand, to stop his hands from shaking.

Jane appeared to be willing to accept his plea of a hangover as an explanation for his behaviour, as she had not contested his claim that it was a drinking bout with Christopher which had kept him up all night. It was hard to know whether she was suspending her intelligence or being too clever by half.

It was hard to know how to phrase an opening remark to Christopher. He was lying, stocking-footed, on a sofa in the picture gallery which ran the length of the top floor of the château. There was a florilegium by his elbow which he appeared to be studying. He seemed smaller in the daylight, and more benign. It was Simeon's hope, as he walked the thirty-four paces from the door that Christopher would be the first to speak. Christopher raised his head and smiled at him but not, perhaps, with the warmth he might have wished for. He shifted his feet a little as Simeon made to sit on the end of his sofa.

They were broad, rounded feet, the balls of which were almost spherical, the toes of which were blunt. It would have been hard for Simeon not to take one of them in his hands, and so he did, moving his fingers against the dry roughness of the cotton, folding his knuckles into the cavity below the toes. Alongside the fear and the excitement he felt a calm which he had never yet encountered as though, by holding this foot, he was absorbing opium through the palms of his hands.

When, at last, Christopher spoke, he did so without taking his eyes from the page beneath him. 'D'you do this sort of thing much, then?' At the end of his sentence he shifted his eyes to the foot that was being manipulated and regarded it neutrally.

Simeon could not make sense of the question or of the tone in which it was spoken; could not think of a dignified reply, except to close the hollow of his hand around an ankle bone.

Christopher said, 'I was having a chat with Jane this morning. She seems a very nice woman.'

The accusing tone made Simeon answer with a note of impatience. 'I wouldn't have married her if I hadn't thought so myself.'

'Nice kids.'

'We do our best.'

'So what's all this about then?'

It was like being up before the headmaster. Simeon breathed deeper in an attempt at breathing more evenly and said, 'I don't know. I honestly don't know. I honestly feel that this is outside my control. I don't know what to do next, if anything.'

'Enabler, enable thyself.'

'For Christ's sake. This isn't easy.'

'I'm glad to hear it. I should hope it isn't.'

Simeon looked as though he was in pain. He said, 'What is all this; this morality all of a sudden? I felt something. I thought there was something going on. Now you're behaving more like someone who caught us at it than the person I was doing it with.'

'Yeah. Perhaps I made a mistake. Maybe I misread things last night. You and Jane seemed hardly to know each other. I assumed you weren't getting on or something.'

'We were tired. It was a long drive.'

'Well, as I say: now that I've spoken to her, properly, I like her. I think she's in love with you. Shagging men who like to think they're straight is one thing. Breaking up marriages isn't my idea of a kick. Last night seemed like a bit of harmless fun at the time. Maybe we should leave it at that.'

'I don't think I can.'

'That's your problem, matey.'

'Don't you feel anything?'

'Fucking Norah, you closets are beyond belief. Look at yourself. You're tall, you're gorgeous, you look as though you've got a big dick and you have. If you sit around with cow eyes and your legs splayed in front of any single gay man he's going to want to fuck your brains out. Well, those were my feelings on the matter anyway. If you want to create a retrospective justification of what went on by imagining that we fell in love with each other then you're on your own, matey. Personally, even if I wanted to get into a relationship, it wouldn't be with someone who lied about something as fundamental as his sexuality. My sympathies are with Jane. With those children.'

'Harriet and James.'

'Goodness me. You even know their names.'

'That's not fair.'

'I think I'd like to have my foot back now, if you've finished with it.'

When Simeon reached the door of the gallery he turned to speak; to say the thing that had formed in thirty-four paces. The acoustics were extraordinary, and his voice was carried the length of the room without him having to raise it, over sofas and tables, between bookcases and fireplaces and outsized portraits of women with long noses. The smooth, neutral accent of the estate agent was cracked as he spoke.

'It's never felt like lying. It's always felt as though I was doing the right thing at the time. It isn't that I don't love her, that I don't want to.'

Christopher's look could not have been more level, more knowing, more cynical.

'Maybe you need help. But not mine. Good luck,' he said.

The stairs, though broad and shallow, induced such a feeling of vertigo in Simeon that he held the banister with two hands, all the way down.

∫

WHEN IN ROME TRY THE GUINNESS

∫

You, in some ways, are not unlike my neighbour. I glare at him every morning. He is a slight, elderly, inoffensive-looking man who has placed a hand-written notice on his door asking that the gate be shut, and he has no idea what he may have done to earn my disapprobation. Perhaps he thinks me a misanthropist, but surely he has heard my cheerful greeting to Muriel downstairs as I pass her in the hall, picking up her Pizzashack leaflets from the doormat, in mules the size, shape and texture of a pair of angora rabbits of exhibition quality, dyed tope. Muriel and I discuss the weather, when it is good, and the plumbing, when it is bad. This being a district of regular habits it is usual that when I open the door Mr Schmit, my neighbour, is closing, carefully, his front gate on his return from the newsagents. Muriel wishes him good morning, and he returns her greeting, and I glare. Because it all happened before I was born he cannot guess that I know about his past.

Once, a long time ago, Muriel asked me why I had taken against Mr Schmit. I considered telling her everything but I couldn't be sure that she would keep it to herself. Muriel has not got a malicious bone in her dressing gown, and her immediate reaction would be to give Mr Schmit a chance to answer the accusation. I don't want to have to hear his side of the story or, worse, to hear him say that it was all a long time ago and he can't remember the details; that he is an old man living in peace and shouldn't the past be left alone. I looked Muriel straight in the eye and told her that I had nothing against the man. She knew, from the tone of my voice, not to ask again.

I don't need to leave the house so early, except to avoid a morning discourse with my lodger, who wakes and comes into the kitchen at 8.25, which is why I like to be out by 8.20. As he works in the evenings and I go to the country at the weekends, the morning is the only time when we are in danger of meeting. I last saw him about two and a half years ago, when he had the 'flu, but that couldn't be helped. Muriel has told me that he has taken to dying his hair and is now a blond person. Why she thinks I should be interested I can't imagine.

They tease me at the office, mistaking my habitual early arrival as an enthusiasm for work. I take this in my usual good-natured way: adjust my spectacles and smile, sometimes even running a hand through my hair, at the risk of being thought flirtatious. It is important that I never let them see that I am aware of their envy, which has been increasing of late. It was tactless, perhaps, to wear my new jacket to work on Tuesday.

Harriet Murphy was the first to say something, having pretended not to notice for half the morning.

'What colour is that supposed to be?' she asked.

'Oatmeal,' I replied, trying not to sound smug.

She immediately feigned a loss of interest but, quick as a flash, I struck home. 'It's from Selfridges,' I added, without a trace of boastfulness.

Muriel was not so parsimonious in her appreciation. She said that she almost hadn't recognised me I had got so elegant, and asked me coyly whether there might not be a young lady on the horizon. Somewhere in all that, the seeds of the possibility of romance were sown. Somewhere in all of that, though we have yet to meet, I began to think of you.

I meant no offence when I said that you were not unlike Mr Schmit. I certainly didn't mean to imply that you have a regrettable past, and I hope that you don't. What I meant is that I am regarding you in a certain way and you have no idea why. I know things about you that you think I can't possibly know. That is my job and it can't be helped. And, like Mr Schmit, if I were to confront you with these things, you would only refute them on some level. Like him, you would be more prepared to believe your own carefully constructed idea of yourself than accept the astute observation of another. As liars we are all at our most successful when in conversation with ourselves.

I, of course, am an exception.

Yesterday I bought new underwear, and this morning I found myself studying my single bed after I had made it up, thinking of replacing it with a double, after all these years. It can't just be on account of the unusually sunny April we are having. If you knew the plans I had for us you would probably run a mile. That is why I am not going to tell you, and you will be glad of it afterwards.

I almost told Muriel about the ad. She has a romantic soul and it is the sort of thing she would have enjoyed hearing about. But today she was agitated about my lodger and there was no opportunity to bring the subject up. She said that she has not seen him enter or leave the house for some time. I said that he was probably on holiday or something. She said that that was what she had thought, at first, but when it went over the fortnight she began to have her doubts. To reassure her I fetched my bank statements, which showed that his rent was being paid into my account as usual.

Not that I would ever have dreamt of opening it, but my conversation with Muriel caused me to hesitate at the door of his room for a fraction of a second. There was an odd and not entirely pleasant smell lingering in that part of the hall. I wrote him a note, pointing out that the weather was now sufficiently mild for him to open his windows from time to time, and slid the note beneath his door, which is our accepted method of communication.

It is fair to say that I am anticipating a measure of excitement at the prospect of meeting you. I have chosen a pub which, though it is centrally located, does not over-charge and serves an excellent cask-condition Real Shandy. Crucially, it is also on the Circle Line, which means that if I am outrageously early for our rendezvous which, knowing me, is not unlikely, I can do a circuit or two on the tube to kill time. I do not like to sit alone in pubs.

I had a nightmare last night in which I was waiting for you in that pub and Mr Schmit, my neighbour, entered, holding a copy of *Time Out*, with my ad circled on the open page. He was not put off by my glare and I had to shout at him. Still he looked at me with importunate eyes, and so I hit him and kicked him, feeling his bones collapse like fresh, dry snow. I wanted blood, not this arid imploding, and became so blind in my anger that I had no option but to wake. With only twenty minutes to go before the alarm it was not worth sleeping again, so I lay in the half dark, thinking of him in his bed in the next house, probably no more than fifteen feet from me, as the crow flies, and I had a surprisingly vivid fantasy of burning him out. Rough justice I know, but what, I ask myself, did God give us the gift of fantasy for if we are not prepared to use it?

I wonder sometimes if you and I will go away together; leave all this and go somewhere quiet, like Isleworth, but then I think of the disadvantages of being outside Zone 2, and revert to my original plan, which is that you come and live here. Do we keep the lodger or not? I need to discuss that sort of thing with you.

He is, I think, a writer of sorts or, at least, he was when he moved in. He was full of it in those days, and intolerably superior, as though being a writer could justify his existence. I do not think he meant to sneer about my job, but I took it a little hard when he opined that a beneficial parasite was still a parasite. It was soon after that that I began to time my breakfast to miss his company. His was the sort of naivity I could do without. We are all trapped inside ourselves, and no amount of writing stories or publishing stories or reading stories is going to change that. Fiction, for those who need it, will never be more that a way of making imprisonment bearable. If my lodger had worked that out for himself he might not still be a waiter in the evenings, in a restaurant with paper serviettes.

I think, with you by my side, we could find a better lodger than that.

I do wish that you would hurry; read my ad and reply. I know that in some respects I have let you down already by taking so many years to work up the courage to place it. It seems to me, in some ways, that I have been saving for this moment. Money, yes, in the first place, though the scope of my investments need never be any concern of yours, and I am sure that you are the sort of person who will not have been imprudent in your own accounting. I could never love a spendthrift. What is more to the point is that I have been saving my luck, in the belief that we are all given only so much. I have never gambled or crossed the road incautiously; never bought so much as a lottery ticket, or travelled in an aeroplane. I have saved my fortune and now the time has come for me to collect it.

And, also, I have been spare with affection. If that has been easier for me than it might be for most, it may be that I have my parents to thank. They are not the kind of people to trouble themselves or others with the burden of emotions. There is a word used too often these days, which I have never heard in that household; a word which the dignity of my parents would not allow, or acknowledge. A word I have been spared the excess of. And though the word love will never come between us, I have a lifetime's affection reserved for you, having never given it, or taken it from another.

I see my parents every weekend when I go down to catalogue my collection, which now stands at two hundred and seventy-four officially, but over a thousand if you count minor varients, which the president of the Society was kind enough to say I was particulary adept at spotting. The collection has to be kept at my parents' house because the air quality is so much better at Tunbridge Wells. My visits have become somewhat ritualised, from my father's usual opening remark of 'Good God is it Saturday already?', to our family Sunday luncheon of scampi-in-a-basket at The Golden Ploughlad, to my unobtrusive leavetaking while my mother has her nap.

I believe that the underlying sanity of my parents' union was founded in the first years of their marriage, during the war. He was taken prisoner at the beginning of 1940, within a fortnight of their wedding, and they heard no more of each other until 1945. They wrote to each other regularly, once a week in my mother's case, but somehow, not a single letter ever got through. It may have been all those words written down and wasted which demonstrated to them the pointlessness of communication. Certainly they have never exchanged a word in my presence, and there is no question but that their marriage is insoluble. They are entirely dependent on one another. My father cannot cook and my mother is allergic to roses.

Being an open-minded man, my father returned from Germany having learned a lot from his captors. He once confided in me that, in his opinion, this country could do with someone with the strength of character to take over and sort things out. That, I remember, was on the day I earned my Duke of Edinburgh Award. 'A fine man,' my father said, twice, being in an unusually loquacious frame of mind.

Not that you need worry that I take after my parents in every respect. By their standards I am a chatty soul though, aside from my exchanges with Muriel, I have not had many opportunities to express this side of my nature. Another thing, you see, that I have been saving for you. The time I have waited before looking for you has, if anything, only given us more to talk about; more to catch up on when we meet. There will be no awkward silences, I can assure you. My life may be a plain one, but it is interesting to a true connoisseur of lives. It was my lodger who told me that once, in the days when he first lived here and was still trying to find a way to broach my confidence. He was not without the occasional, valuable observation.

In the beginning, before we settled down to our present, more comfortable way of living together, I was kindness itself to that man. I am, you see, one of nature's givers. That, of course, leaves you open to all kinds of abuse, and I find I need to be constantly on my guard against those who would take advantage of my generosity. Beggars, the so-called homeless, are one of the things one has to be wary of. I mean, what did they ever give anyone; what did they ever give to society? No, it is people like me who give everything. I pay my taxes, and that is something in which I don't even have a choice. Just thinking about this makes me angry.

Neither did my lodger appreciate what I tried to do for him. When he told me he was a writer I told him my most interesting anecdote; the one about my neighbour, and the extraordinary coincidence by which I discovered his secret past. It is a story I never tire of telling, though I seldom seem to get the opportunity.

It was at about the time that I first bought this maisonette. If I remember rightly it was the same day as that on which I fell out with my first lodger. She had eaten an apple from the fruit basket. 'What did you do that for?' I said. 'They had only been there a week. They were still fresh. They didn't need using up.'

By the blank incomprehension with which she was looking at me I could see that we were never going to get along.

If she could not grasp as simple a principle as when a fruit should be eaten and when it should be left on display there was no hope. Luckily, she left of her own accord before I got round to giving her notice.

I digress, I know, but my present lodger showed a great deal of interest in that part of the story, although not enough to make up for his lack of appreciation of the rest of it. He even wanted to know what sort of apple it had been, and when I told him, he laughed. In any case, the story: At that time Jacqueline Barry still worked in the office, before her nerves forced her into early retirement. I would not say that we were great friends, poor Jacqueline seemed to have a problem in dealing with people, but I would pass the time of day with her once in a while, and on that day I was telling her all about my little drama with the fruit-gobbling lodger and saying how pleased I was, in general, with my new home, when she suddenly turned towards me, put down the magazine she was reading, and said, 'Where did you say you lived?'

'White City.'

'No, the name of the road.' She said it irritably but, with hindsight, I know what the cause was.

'Offaly Close.'

'What number Offaly Close?' The blood was draining from her face.

'Twenty-nine.'

She muttered an unladylike expletive, and then composed herself sufficiently to ask whether there was a very old man living next-door.

'Mr Schmit,' I said. 'He looks like an old Nazi in hiding, but he seems very nice.'

'My sweet Lord,' she said, closing her eyes for a moment and putting her right hand to the cross which dangled from the folds of her camel turtleneck.

'Do you know him then?'

'I was married to him,' she said. Her eyes were glazed as

she spoke, as though she was unconscious of her audience. Not that I minded. I am a very good listener, given the chance, and someone with something of real interest to say. She continued: 'It was a long time ago, just after the war. I wasn't more than a child, really. He was older. It was terrible. I married him because I had nothing, and because I had nothing I couldn't escape from him. Eventually I found myself a job, and the same day I told him I was leaving. He said that I couldn't and I said that he couldn't stop me. Do you know, we had two irons in that house and he wouldn't let me take one of them with me. He said I had no right to it because it belonged to the marriage.'

She shook herself, and looked at me as though she had just noticed my presence, and said that she had better get back to work, and she picked up her magazine and made a great show of reading it.

The lodger, when I related this gem of a story to him, said, 'So that's it? Two irons?'

I would say that any difficulty there has been between us began at that moment. I had as good as bared my soul to the man. I had never spoken so long or so freely to another. But I learned my lesson. Trust, also, I have been saving for your arrival.

We'll have no need of lodgers, you and I. We will laugh together from behind the curtains, overhearing Mr Schmit and his pathetic attempts to be nice to Rodrigo, the Spanish boy from number thirty-three. Eventually, one day, I might bring you to the country to see the collection. I'm sure my mother would be pleased to give you tea, if we bring a cake. She is partial to Battenburg.

The lodger will have to go. This evening I arrived home to notice that the smell was no better. He had returned my note and had Sellotaped a tiny square of card to the top right-hand corner. The card was illustrated with a drawing of a penguin and had slightly serrated edges as though it had been torn from something. Above it was written, 'Eat this'. Below it, 'See God'. Across the body of the letter, looped through my words, he had scrawled, 'When In Rome Try The Guinness'.

∫

THE LAST INNOCENCE OF SIMEON

∫

Interior, bathroom, too bright for comfort. Thinking that if you tried to divide the world into those who were capable of falling in love and those who were not you'd have your work cut out for you. How would you tell? More often than not the subjects themselves, if they were honest, would have to tell you that they didn't know whether they had the propensity for falling in love or, merely, a desire for it. Thinking that if people realised how little they knew or could know about themselves they'd give up and go somewhere else. Perhaps that is what they do. Perhaps that is why, most of the time, when you attempt conversation with someone you get the feeling that you are talking to their answering machine. What on earth is making you think this way, at this hour of the morning? Love and life: you'll be contemplating death next. One of those mornings that happen often enough, when you step into the bathroom and the image reflected sets you thinking; when the face blearing back seems to have been sprayed with ugly in the night; when the tits are not quite as squared off as you'd like to think they are, considering the hours you work on them; when, let's face it, the frustration of not being able to admire yourself makes you philosophical. Now, you've caught yourself out, wallowing in the shallows. You catch your eye in the glass, as you would catch the eye of a conspirator, and it makes you grin.

Mourning not weeping. In his first love letter he said it was a smile that would turn pearls to cream. I can't see it myself but then, even now, I don't think I am in love with myself to anywhere near the degree that Ewan was in love with me. And then, after all these years of studying this face and scowling at it and pouting at it and practising handsomeness from all the angles, it wasn't until recently that I caught myself smiling. In his first love letter Ewan wrote a page and three-quarters about the smile alone, in his flying handwriting, the tail of one letter splashing across the body of another; the cross of a t travelling the page, in his passion. Would this be the smile that Ewan had seen, or is there another dimension to a smile you'd turn on the beloved?

Smile you bugger, and get it right. In another ten years the handsomeness will be gone and you'll only have the smile to fall back on. Now you're laughing at yourself, in the mirror. That is a new development. Laughing loud enough to wake the trade, stretched in the bed beyond, through the open door, left open so I could glance at his flesh among the sheets, between strokes of the razor. Not a beauty perhaps, but sweet, and tactile, and a dick you could exercise a horse on. Could it be that I am becoming a size queen? Ewan wasn't exactly hung to his knees. In his first love letter he apologised for it, not knowing that as far as I was concerned everything on him and in him was perfect. He was so tentative in the beginning that I thought he must be backing off. I avoided him, to save my dignity, and that was the occasion of the letter. He sent a typed version with the handwritten; a translation, afraid that any word might be misread, so precisely had he chosen the words he used: pearls to cream. Not Dear Simeon, but Simeon; not with love, but love; no date at the top, but the day of the week: Wednesday.

Do I think of him too much? Afraid that the memory might fade; that I might, one day, think a whole paragraph without a phrase of his mixed somewhere in it; that I might spend a whole night, some night, with another man without once feeling Ewan's breath on the side of my face in a moment of distraction; that I might smell good coffee or K-Y and rubber or Chanel scent or burning milk on the stovetop and not think of him. He made me promise not to mourn him, and it is rare that I need to weep for him. There is little sadness in his haunting. Long ago he was forgiven for, having taught me to live, dying.

This one, on the bed, the sheets draped and undraped over him as if he had woken and taken the time to arrange them while my back was turned, who knows what this one is, beyond the fact that he is a sybarite, with the currency to earn his pleasures? We passed the same breath back and forth between our lungs until we were dizzy and high with the lack of oxygen. We flew and roared and coated ourselves in layers of sperm until our stomachs crackled when we moved and, now and then, we'd lean back and stare at each other with frank admiration, and one of us would say something shamelessly jingoistic about the potency of our race, and laugh at the ludicrousness of two Paddies picking each other up in preference to all the Action Men in the East Village. His name is Eric. We met in the Crowbar and I liked the way he smiled at me. The paddock-sized dick was a bonus.

Inside myself, after all these decades. Inside myself for the first time since infancy. I won't dramatise it. I won't say it was Ewan who put me here, in my happiness. But it was Ewan who showed that the happiness of an infant was possible, for someone who could be so unselfconscious as an infant; that it is not a matter of being loved, but of knowing that you are lovable.

Sluice water over the scum of bristle that laces the basin. A beard is such a disproportionately fecund thing. Think also of Eric's choking pleasure at the grating of that bristle on his rectum. Should I brush my teeth, or would that be gaining an unfair advantage over him when I poke him awake, with coffee? Check by the ears and nostrils for stray wisps of Noxzema, and tweak the glass rod that opens the blinds a fraction, the better to see. I love the light in this city. If you say that to a native he will look at you a little strangely for a moment, before agreeing with you. Plainly, you can become immune to the light here. If that ever happens it will be time to move on. There are enough exciting places in the world and no excuse not to be excited by the place you are standing in.

Brush the teeth, for the comfort of a clean mouth. A twinge in the gums, and a little panic at the possibility of a mouth ulcer, but there is no sign of anything nasty. Not that it should make any difference, but last night Eric made a confession of rare generosity. He was only the second man I have ever known to have had the consideration to do that and Ewan, of course, was the first. It was after we got back here, at maybe one this morning, before we had done more than kiss. There was no need for him to have told me and he took a risk by doing so. There are some, even in these days of putative enlightenment, who would have showed him the door in the light of that knowledge.

'You don't mind?' he said, as I unbuttoned his flies.

'Why should I? The only difference between us is that you know that you're positive and I don't. If I'd had a test yesterday I still couldn't be sure. It isn't going to affect what we do or what we don't do. People like me are a bigger risk than you are.'

I don't know if he heard half of what I was saying, muffled through the silken bulges of a mouthful of genitalia; trailed off towards the end as his tumescence took priority; punctuated in ungrammatical places by his grunts of encouragement. He pulled me to my feet and kissed me.

'My turn,' he said, slithering down.

He has the sort of body that doesn't look much at first, and suddenly he is over you, a dick in each hand, both arms pumping, muscles bursting through his skin and a filthy expression on his face, and the sight of him alone could make you come, and did. I thought at first he was laughing at me, at the sight of me shuddering and squirting, until his own glutinous arc landed on my shoulder and I understood that his delight was his own. I've never before seen anyone laugh like that at a moment of crisis. It makes me wonder what sort of creature I have in my bed. I could stay here all day and watch the tempting way he sleeps, and wonder all those things that occur to you after a night with a man you like the smell and taste and smile of. Will he stay and will I want him to stay? I love this moment, before a man you hardly know wakes up, when you can think that you might be in love with him, knowing in the back of your mind that you can impress him with a home-cooked breakfast and send him on his way.

Would he stay and would I love him? Why is it that as soon as you have decided that you are happy to be single, have never, to your knowledge, been happier, you find yourself entertaining domestic fantasies; entertaining men with that store-cupboard glint in their eyes? Not in his, perhaps, but then I hardly know him. Or do I know as much as there is, as much as is significant? He seemed disarmingly honest. We talked, muttered confidences to each other as the sweat dried, our tongues loosened, perhaps, by being with someone who spoke our own form of this language. His mouth, full and lush in repose became, in talking, wired; a hard, undulating line that curled and straightened about his teeth. I devoted at least as much concentration to watching his mouth as to hearing his words; flirted with alarmingly romantic ideas while watching it.

'You are,' I said, 'an extraordinary man.'

'Being extraordinary,' he said, 'is relatively easy. I tried ordinary once and it was a bitch.'

While I was laughing I thought of all the years I had wasted in pursuit of ordinariness. Spent not wasted. You cannot accuse, even in your own mind, your children of having been a waste of part of your life.

I confessed my past to him.

'Where are they now?' he asked, in a voice too idle for accusation.

'Jersey. That's how come I'm here, originally. Jane, my ex, was offered a job over here, one that was too good to turn down, so I upped sticks and followed them. I know what it's like to be that age and not have a father. The only big problem at the moment is that they're beginning to get accents. It'll be a bit of a liability for them if they have to go through life sounding like Americans.'

'A cruel and unusual punishment,' he said. 'So what do you do anyway?'

I love that. I love it when a man who has just been ferreting deliriously in your rudest bits has to ask you the most basic questions about yourself; things that people you wouldn't even undress in front of have known for years.

'I'm a hack. I write about property. I used to be an estate agent in the eighties, but then the crash happened and there was more money to be made by writing about houses not being sold than by not selling them. It took a while to break into it over here, but I had good credentials. Well, credentials that looked good from this distance. What are you at yourself?'

'Guess. Irishman abroad. It has to be navvy or novelist doesn't it?'

'So which is it?'

'Both, unfortunately. But so far I've only managed to gain recognition as a navvy. Luckily I look cute in sawn-offs with a layer of brick dust, so there's no problems on the entertainment front. Sometimes I feel like giving up on the novelist thing, and sometimes it's the only thing that keeps me going. I want to be published before I croak.'

'Why?' I had asked the question before I realised how crass it was.

'I don't know. Because I want to find out how much of me is self-delusion and how much of me is worth anything. Because I'm promiscuous by nature and I want to fuck with the minds of complete strangers. Because I want to be less afraid of dying. Because, if nothing else, I think that being a writer must be a complete blast. The ultimate fuck-off profession. I want to know what it's like to be as free as that. As shameless as that.'

'And words? Don't they come into it?'

'This is not,' he said, warily, 'the sort of conversation I have with every shag.'

'I have a little second-hand experience,' I said. 'I used to live with a writer.'

'What happened there?'

'He died.'

The question hung, and I let it hang for a moment, and answered it for him just before he had to ask it.

'No,' I said. 'Not the usual. He had a heart attack. He cheated the virus. He'd been positive for years; was positive when I met him. We were all worked up about how we were going to handle it when the count started to drop, and then the fucker goes and keels over on me with a heart attack. He was fit enough, or he seemed to be, and doing nothing strenuous at the time – hadn't touched the poppers for years, even when he was off his tits and screaming to be fucked, backing into me like a mare in season. No. He was just sitting at his computer. The last word he wrote was "And". Just that. "And". There was no other word on the screen, so it was obviously the beginning of something. It was his nightmare, that he would die with something unfinished, like the man with the sorrel filly in *La Peste*. "And". You couldn't have something more unfinished than that, if you tried.

'I wouldn't worry too much about getting yourself published if I was you. I've seen that racket at close quarters and I'd rather be a navvy if I had the choice. Though Ewan always claimed that choice didn't come into it.'

'Ewan?' he said. 'Ewan who?'

'Ewan Strong.'

'Fuck me pink,' he said.

Then he did what a lot of them did when they found out that Ewan Strong had been my lover. He looked down at my dick and closed his hand around it as though it was a talisman; the totem which had plugged the man who had described our lives. I tried not to react; to tell myself that I would do the same in the same circumstances. To be honest, I was jealous, in a small way, as you are always jealous of the love of others for your lover, no matter what form that love takes.

To change the context of his action I pushed his knees up either side of his face and gave him a big slap across the backside.

'You're into a bit of CP then?' he said.

'No,' I said. 'Proud to be vanilla.'

'Good,' he said. 'It's the reluctant ones that squeal the loudest.'

'No fucking way,' I said.

'We'll see about that.' He cast his eyes back towards the palm of his hand, where a vulcanisation was betraying the excitement I had denied, and then, as if he was holding the erection at arm's length, he said, 'What's it like fucking a woman?'

The question seemed stark in the circumstances.

'Fine,' I said. 'All right. Wonderful, sometimes. Easier, from a technical point of view, in some senses. Not all that different, in reality. I don't know. Why are you asking?'

He had dropped his hold of my dick and was looking at it in an odd way, as though it had been contaminated by encounters with women, when only moments before he had been revering it as though encounters with Ewan had sanctified it. I had the feeling he might have shuddered had I not been watching him so closely.

'I don't understand how anyone could. It doesn't seem natural, somehow. A gay man doing that.'

I'm afraid I got schoolmarmish with him at that point. 'So? Fine. You, maybe, were always sure of what you were, maybe. I had to be certain, and perhaps I spent years codding myself, but I thought, for a long time, that I was doing the things that made me happy. I wasn't revolted by straight sex. I liked it. I thought sex was only about pleasure until the first time I fucked a man. And I was nearly thirty when that happened.'

'And then?' he said, with a challenge in his tone that was not attractive. 'What was so different then, in this catalytic fuck? I'm sorry, I find these conversion stories hard to swallow.'

'What can I say?'

'What it was like. What happened. Explain to me, because I've never known anything else; explain the love of men.'

I would have told him that he was asking too much, but he knew that already. I had to remind myself that this inquisition would not be so pressing if he didn't want me to acquit myself.

'It's like drugs,' I said, 'or religion, or death, or fact. Once you've done it there's no substitute. There's no going back. It's like knowledge and once you have it you can't cod yourself that you don't know. Times I find a last wisp of innocence somewhere about me, like going to a bar and, after half an hour of nonchalant cruising, seeing a bit of shaving cream by your ear when you glance in the mirror. Shreds of innocence are the hardest to live with, and the thing about innocence is that it's all or nothing. You can only be happy at either end of the process. Am I talking shite?'

'I like you talking shite,' he said. 'Naif philosophy is such a turn-on.' He bent my head over and began to lick the back of my neck, arching his body tight until the end of his cock was banging on my nostril.

To see him now, seamless and breathing softly. He knows,

I think, that I am watching him; knows it whether he is sleeping or not. He has that attitude of an animal that knows he is being admired. His skin is twitching to be touched. Who knows what he is, beyond what he has said he is? I remember more of what I told him than of what he told me, but then my stories were the ones I know more intimately.

Interior, bathroom, daylight. Shaved and teeth brushed and almost fully awake now after nearly half an hour of grimacing in the mirror and indulging his mind with a puddle of consciousness, Simeon stepped into the shower and let the streams run between his skin and the previous night's carapace of dried sperm; smiling at the feel of the soap and the illusion of cleanliness.

The expression on his face would lead you to believe that he had just fallen in love or, failing that, and very unlikely I grant you, that he was happy in his own right.

Eric Hanlon in the bed, on hearing the beat of the shower, turned himself over and arranged himself to be as enticing as possible, one leg bent for a Caravaggian glimpse of the buttocks, lower arms hidden as if he might be tied, the manège of an organ stirring obligingly, but no more than you would expect of a functioning young man with a full bladder at that hour of the day. He liked that. He liked being the slut in bed, reeking to heaven of two men; apparently asleep, and the feel of a clean, slightly damp man, smelling of water, climbing over him tentatively, gently playing with him as though not to wake him. He liked to hear the first growl of satisfaction from one who was trying to be silent, and feel the first flutter of a tongue that couldn't help itself, on the head of his cock for preference. He liked, above all, the idea that he was irresistible.

This one, whatever he called himself, was taking his time in the bathroom. Perhaps it would not be a bad thing to devote this hiatus to an effort to remember his name. Sim Sim something, Simeon. It could be worse. He had spent the night with a man called Ashley once. The strain of not saying fiddledee had almost overwhelmed him.

He could smell the water before he felt the first drip from Simeon's wet hair. He waited to be touched but, instead, felt a slight trembling in the bed. The filthy bugger was jerking off over him. It was important not to wriggle at this stage; to maintain the illusion. The first fleck splashed on his throat, the second slid down his hip-bone, the main consignment was delivered to his balls. It was hell not responding to it, and half the pleasure.

He woke officially when Simeon brought the coffee. He put his hand between his legs, brought it back beneath his nose, inhaled and grinned.

'What's been going on here then?'

'Sorry,' Simeon said, without bothering to look too sorrowful. 'I'll make it up to you.'

'You betcha you will.'

'How's the coffee?'

'Good. Spoiling the trade, you are.'

'That means something else over here. Trade.'

'I know. A lot of things do.'

'They say "trick". I don't like that word. It sounds dishonest. It sounds as if you wouldn't look him in the eye after you'd fucked him.'

Feeling it was a bit early in the morning for the semantics of gay slang, but not wanting to furrow the atmosphere, Eric said nothing.

'So,' Simeon said, 'let's get the ghoulish exile bit out of the way. Which tit of the Sainted Sow did you suck on? The only thing I can tell from your accent is that you probably went to UCD.'

'Very good,' Eric said. 'Top marks. The only thing I can tell from yours is that you weren't long in losing it. You won't have heard of where I'm from. It's a place called Mowlinstown, in the middle of nowhere.'

'Mowlinstown? Mowlinstown on the New Line? Beyond Pollick Cross? What's your second name?'

'Hanlon.'

'Well fuck you pink and back again. What age are you?'

The Hanlon boy was too stunned by Simeon's reaction and knowledge to do more than answer the questions he was given, and search the face in front of him for indications of its provenance.

'Twenty-six,' he said.

'That's it, so. You look older. You would have been no more than a scrap when I left. What's Maggie doing with herself these days?'

'She got a job with Aer Lingus. Teaching the young wans to hand out boiled sweets while balancing half a pound of make-up on each eyelid. She married some tosser from Cavan with a chip on his shoulder about poofs, so I don't see much of her when I go home. Who the fuck are you anyway?'

'Simmy.' The old form of his name almost creaked in the disinterment.

Eric went white and said something that sounded like 'fffph'.

'I know,' Simeon said. 'Fuck you pink.'

Eric pulled the sheet over his mid-section as if his nudity were suddenly immodest, at which Simeon smiled, at which Eric began to laugh. He laughed for ten minutes at a stretch and then again, in shorter bursts.

'I remember you, now that I think about it,' Simeon said. 'You were a disgusting child. A yard of snot in your nose and always trying to feck money out of my pockets.'

'I was probably trying to get a feel of your dick.'

'At that age?'

'Not all of us had to wait until we were thirty to work out what was what.'

'So much for innocence.'

An anger of some kind became evident when Eric next

spoke. 'There's more than one kind of innocence. And more than one way of being fucked up by whatever innocence afflicts you.'

'What's wrong? What's the matter?'

'Don't say that like that. Don't ask me that as if you know me. I hate the way you're so complacent. Maggie still talks about you now and again and says you were a complacent cunt, when she has drink on her. You haven't changed much.'

'I'm sorry. It seemed the thing to do at the time.'

There was a time when Simeon's face could cave in sorrow and still be a thing to look at. Now, unhappiness made him look middle-aged, and would for years to come, until he gained the beauty of the old. 'I don't understand,' he said.

'Welcome to the human race.' There was a kindness in Eric's voice when he said that, and a viciousness when he followed it with, 'I knew Mrs Doyle. I used to help her in the garden when she got frail.'

'Knew?'

'She isn't dead yet, from what I've heard. She used to talk about you a lot, and speculate how you were getting on. The odd postcard wouldn't have hurt.'

'I hardly knew the woman.'

'She knew you. There was always an envelope on her dresser with your full name on it. I looked in it once and it was full of old money. I didn't like to ask her what was at the bottom of that one. Though we were close. She was my first fag hag. She knew what I was about and she made things easier for me. She's the first I visit when I'm home.'

'So that's why you're angry.'

'No. I'm angry for all kinds of reasons. It doesn't take much to bring it out. I'm angry because I fancied you like fuck until I found out who you were.'

'Now?'

'I don't know. Years ago I used to dream of you, and think you had everything. By coincidence you did. How many men could hope to have children and Ewan Strong in the same lifetime? When I let you jerk off over me this morning it was because you were a fantasy man, perversely enough, not unlike the fantasies I used to have in Mowlinstown when I'd think of you and masturbate. Now that I know what you are, this morning feels more like molestation than a game. Now I almost hate you and it's too soon for me to explain it.'

'I'm sorry.'

'Don't say that.'

Simmy reached out towards him, inhaling as he did so, and so becoming aware of the smell of the man before his fingertips lighted on his shoulder. Eric would have liked to flinch, but didn't. They kissed, like lovers; like a kiss of seduction.

Simeon spoke. He used only the one word, and it was the last word between them for some time.

'Stay,' he said.

Acknowledgments

SALTHILL first appeared in the *Irish Times*. DOYLE'S CROSS, AFTER THE CONQUERING HERO and THE STICKY CAR-PET were all broadcast on BBC Radio 4 (the first two under the titles LEAVING DOYLE'S CROSS and AFTER THE GAR-DEN). HOOK HEAD and KENWOOD CHEF were published in *Image*. KILBRIDE and THE ROWER were published in *Scripsi* (Australia); THE ROWER also appeared in *Glimmer Train* (USA) and *Best Short Stories 1994*. RINGSEND was first published in *New Woman*, LEGACY in the *Daily Telegraph* and HANDSOME MEN ARE SLIGHTLY SUNBURNT in *Cosmopolitan* and subsequently *The Best of Cosmo Short Fiction*. Some of these stories have been slightly altered since their original publication.

This collection owes a great deal to David Miller, who is a crusader, not only on behalf of these, but for the short story in general.